YELL . . . OR SOMETHING!

There was no point in trying to explain. It wasn't only that I was bored in my new home. I wanted to go back to Seattle because my new home didn't come even close to the new life I'd wanted.

I went home to a brief discussion with Will and Mom about the incident at school, and then to a long evening of clocks ticking and Mrs. Brier slamming pans around in the kitchen. It sounds stupid, but I would have felt loved if someone—anyone—had yelled at me.

I was living in the dead zone.

Other Avon Flare Books by
Jean Thesman

COULDN'T I START OVER?
THE LAST APRIL DANCERS
WAS IT SOMETHING I SAID?
WHO SAID LIFE IS FAIR?

THE WHITNEY COUSINS Trilogy
AMELIA
ERIN
HEATHER

THE WHITNEY COUSINS

HEATHER

JEAN THESMAN

AN AVON  FLARE BOOK

THE WHITNEY COUSINS: HEATHER is an original publication of Avon Books. This work has never before appeared in book form.

AVON BOOKS
A division of
The Hearst Corporation
105 Madison Avenue
New York, New York 10016

First Avon Flare Printing: May 1990

AVON FLARE TRADEMARK REG. U.S. PAT. OFF. AND IN OTHER COUNTRIES, MARCA REGISTRADA, HECHO EN U.S.A.

Printed in the U.S.A.

RA   10 9 8 7 6 5 4 3 2

Chapter 1

Thought for the day: To be happy, you must expect the best, prepare for the worst, and never leave tuna fish sandwiches and your gym socks in your locker over the weekend.

> Harold Z. Zoppler, Principal
> Fox Crossing High School

The Labor Day holiday when I was fifteen was the happiest day of my life and also the saddest day. All my dreams about having my own family had come true— and my worst nightmares about being separated from my cousin Amelia had come true, too.

We spent that last afternoon in Amelia's bedroom, packing my stuff. I'd been with her family for a month— I always spent August with them—but now, instead of going back to the apartment Mom and I had shared for most of my life, I was moving to a new town with my new stepfather and stepsister. My mother had remarried a week before. I was leaving Seattle for Fox Crossing and starting my sophomore year in high school there the next day. I wasn't nervous about that. Well, not very nervous. That's because I knew exactly how everything was going to be—perfect.

"Are you going to pack these awful things or throw them out?" my cousin Amelia asked, holding up my old straw sandals with one hand and reaching for her waste basket with the other.

"Throw them out," I said. "No, stick them in that

1

box over there in the corner." I sat back on my heels and took a good look around. "I hope I haven't forgotten anything."

Jamie, her ten-year-old brother, was watching from the doorway. He has light brown hair, like Amelia and me, but his eyes are brown like his mother's. We have what Amelia calls "Whitney eyes." They're grass green.

"Come and hug me good-bye," I said when I saw him. "Mom and Dr. Carver will be here any minute." Dr. Carver was my new stepfather, an English professor at the college in Fox Crossing.

Jamie's face turned red. "I don't hug girls."

"You hug Mimi all the time," I teased.

"Five-year-old sisters don't count," he said. He stuck his hands in his pockets and tried to look casual. "You'll come back to Seattle sometime, won't you?"

"Of course!" I said. "I'll always spend August here, and I'll come back other times, too. I'll only be a couple of hours away."

"It seems as far as Alaska to me," Amelia said. She rolled up my pajamas and stuffed them into the last box we were packing. "I can't imagine getting along at school without you."

Suddenly both of us were crying. "You've got friends there," I wailed. "I don't know anybody at my new school. I hardly even know my stepfather and stepsister."

Amelia hugged me until my ribs hurt. "If it's too awful, ask your mom if you can move back in with us."

I shook my head. "No. I've wanted my own family for as long as I can remember. It'll just take getting used to, that's all."

"Won't you miss us?" Mimi, my youngest cousin, was standing in the doorway, her big eyes filled with tears.

I picked her up and swung her around. "How can I

2

miss you when I'm going to steal you and take you with me?''

She laughed and squealed at the same time, and forgot about crying. I saw my aunt and uncle watching from the hall. Something about their faces told me that my time was up.

"Is Mom here?" I was trying to swallow the lump in my throat.

"They're opening up the back of their station wagon," Aunt Ellen said. "They'll be coming inside in just a minute."

I blinked back tears. "I'm done packing. Uncle Jock, will you help me carry my stuff down to the driveway?"

He tried to laugh. "I ought to say no, because I don't want to lose you," he said.

"Heather, say you won't go!" Six-year-old Cassie ran down the hall. Her glasses were hanging crooked as usual, and her eyes were red. "Say that you'll stay with us!"

I put Mimi down and bent to hug Cassie. "Don't you want me to have my own dad and sister?"

"But you've got us!" she insisted. "You don't need a new dad or a new sister!"

I saw my mother at the head of the stairs with Dr. Carver right behind her. She smiled but didn't say anything.

Aunt Ellen picked Cassie up, telling her that if I didn't leave right then, I wouldn't reach my new home in time for dinner.

The next minutes were too awful to describe. I was still crying when we headed north on the freeway, and I couldn't bring myself to look back at the Seattle skyline.

Pull up your socks and quit acting like a baby, I told myself. You're getting what you always wanted.

I leaned over the back of Dr. Carver's seat, cleared

3

my throat and said, "Did you enjoy your trip, Dr. Carver?"

"We had a wonderful time," he said quietly. "But California is too hot for me. I'll be glad to see home again." He glanced over at Mom, and then added, "Heather, I'd like it if you called me Dad. Or Will. After all, we're family now."

My own father had died soon after I was born, but I wouldn't have felt right calling someone else Dad. "I'll call you Will," I said. "Is your daughter going to be home when we get there?"

"Tracey told me on the phone this morning that she was going to a picnic with her boyfriend's family," Will said, "so she might not be home when we arrive. But she said she'd found some blooming heather to put in your room as a welcome."

Having an older sister was great. I'd met Tracey briefly at Mom's wedding and I was looking forward to seeing her again. She was seventeen, a senior in high school, and she had already promised in a letter that she'd introduce me around at school so I'd feel comfortable there as soon as possible.

It took longer than two hours to reach Fox Crossing because of the holiday traffic. I saw the town first from the top of a hill. It was neat and pretty, surrounded by green fields with woods in the distance. But it was awfully small.

We pulled into a circular driveway and stopped. I'd been hoping for a big, old, comfortable place like Amelia's. Instead, I was moving into a house that looked like something in a magazine, and I knew that I'd be afraid to walk on the floors without removing my shoes first.

"Here we are, Heather," Will said. "Run inside and tell Mrs. Brier that we're home. We'll bring the luggage in."

I got out of the station wagon and climbed the steps slowly. I'd met Mrs. Brier, the housekeeper, at the wedding, and I'd tried hard to forget about her.

Before I could open the door, it swung open, and the small, scowling woman said, "Dinner's ready. Your room is at the end of the hall upstairs, on the right. Wash your hands and come back down immediately."

Without waiting for a reply, Mrs. Brier bustled out to the station wagon. She reminded me of one of the awful housekeepers you read about in Gothic novels, but she wasn't wearing a black dress with her long gray hair in a bun. She was dressed in slacks and a sweater, and her hair was orange and frizzy.

I marched inside and up the stairs, determined to be agreeable. But I was afraid that it'd never feel like home here. Everything was too polished and perfect—the house looked unused.

And it was too quiet. I could actually hear a clock ticking downstairs and another ticking upstairs.

We had dinner in an enormous dining room. The three of us sat at one end of a long table and ate chicken from antique china, using heavy silver.

At Amelia's, we ate at a big, round table and used mismatched china and stainless steel flatware. And at Amelia's we talked and laughed all through each meal.

At the Carver house, we ate almost in silence. Mom and Will exchanged a couple of quiet comments about the garden. Mrs. Brier served the food, along with lots of sullen looks directed at me.

I didn't dare let myself think. This wasn't starting out like my favorite fantasy.

Tracey and her boyfriend arrived while we were having dessert in Will's den. She was tall and thin and she wore glasses like her father. Her hair was a soft, mousy brown like his, too. Her boyfriend, John Hay, was even taller and his glasses were even thicker. He was in col-

lege already, although I suspected that he was only sev
enteen, like Tracey. Both of them smiled at me and
asked me how I liked Fox Crossing. I said it was a pretty
town.

"Do you like to play chess?" John asked me.

"I don't know how," I told him, shrugging uncom
fortably.

"I'll teach you," Tracey said.

I smiled to show gratitude, but the last thing I wanted
to learn at that moment was chess.

"Let's put on some music," Tracey said, and
cheered up. I'd seen the big stereo system and longed
to try some of my tapes on it. Tracey slipped a compac
disc into the player, and I heard symphony music pou
out.

John sat down next to the fireplace and began talking
to Mom and Will about some unusual bird he and Tra
cey had seen at the picnic that afternoon. Mrs. Brie
brought in lemonade and cookies before she went home
We listened to music for an hour and then John left and
Tracey took me upstairs for "girl talk."

Her idea of "girl talk" was to ask me what subject
planned to major in when I started college. I felt like an
idiot because until then I'd never given it much thought

She was nice, really nice. And she was trying very
hard to be a good big sister to me. But when I crawled
into bed that night, I cried myself to sleep because I was
so lonely. And homesick.

What had happened to all my fantasies? I had known
all my life exactly the sort of family I'd have someday
I had daydreamed every detail. The life I wanted wasn'
so unusual. My cousin Amelia's plain, ordinary, good
natured family was exactly right. Their comfortabl
house was like a million others. They were so averag
that you could see them on TV any day.

But this wasn't the right family or the right house.

6

The next morning Tracey walked the half mile to school with me. As soon as we entered the building, two girls stopped dead in their tracks and stared at me.

"Is there something wrong with the way I look?" I whispered to Tracey. "They're staring at me."

She looked around vaguely. "That's because you're new here. I know them. They're sophomores like you. Let's talk to them."

They were still staring and my imagination went wild. Was my hair standing on end? Was there a hole in my skirt that I couldn't see? Had I suddenly become the ugliest person in the universe?

"Hi, you're Micky Logan, aren't you?" Tracey said to the girl with short, dark hair.

The girl nodded, still gaping at me.

"This is my new stepsister, Heather Whitney," Tracey said. "She just moved here yesterday."

Micky grinned then. "Hi, Heather." She gestured toward the other girl. "This is Sandy Graham."

The girl with long black hair smiled, too. Then both girls looked at each other and laughed.

"What's wrong?" I asked. "You've been staring at me ever since I came through the door."

They both laughed harder then. Tracey looked puzzled, but she only shrugged. "Sophomores have fun," she said.

A woman came out of the school office, saw Tracey, and beckoned to her. Tracey excused herself and followed the woman through the door. The two girls looked at me and I looked at them.

"I don't believe this," Micky said, shaking her head.

"Neither do I," Sandy said. "Heather, where are you from?"

"Seattle," I told them.

"You aren't by any chance related to the Worth's, are you? The Worth family here in Fox Crossing?"

7

"I never even heard of them," I said. "Why?"

"I really don't believe what I'm seeing," Sandy said to Micky.

"What are you seeing?" I shouted. "Tell me! I can't stand it. Am I weird? Have I grown an extra head or what? What's wrong with me?"

A guy walked up to us. "Wow," he said when he saw me. "Wow."

"This is Thad Shipton," Sandy said.

"Wow," I said crossly to him. Ordinarily I would have been pleased to meet a nice-looking blond boy with clear blue eyes, but he was staring, too, and I was getting awfully tired of being examined like a bug on a windowsill.

"Who is she?" he asked Sandy. "This is amazing."

"She's Heather Whitney, from Seattle. Do you believe it?"

"I sure want to," he said, grinning at me. "You can never have too much of a good thing. Get it, Sandy? Too much? Too as in T-W-O?"

"I've had enough of this and I'm going to the office to register," I said. "You kids can go stare at each other."

I walked away but they followed me. "Please don't be angry, and please don't go in the office yet," Micky begged. "Come with us to the student lounge. There's something you've got to see."

"What?" I asked suspiciously.

"Oh boy," Thad said, grinning. "I can hardly wait. Heather, before you go in, would you promise me something?"

"No," I said. But I couldn't resist. "What?"

"No matter what happens—I mean, even if you go into shock—will you promise that you won't move back to Seattle?"

"Why?" I demanded.

8

"Because I want to see you coming and going around Fox Crossing High," he said, and then he laughed.

The girls were laughing, too, but I wasn't. Without knowing how, I had made myself ridiculous in the eyes of this boy, and I didn't like it one bit.

"Come on," Micky said, and she grabbed my hand. "The lounge is straight down the hall. You're going to love this."

"What am I going to love?" I asked. I had an awful feeling that I was going to end up embarrassed by something, and I wasn't sure I could handle it on the first day in a new school. Where was Tracey? How could she have gone off and left me with strangers?

They led me down the hall and through double doors into the student lounge. Thad trailed behind, grinning.

"Now shut your eyes and let me take you around the corner," Sandy said.

"No," I said.

"Be a sport," Sandy said. "Micky, you go ahead and, you know, set up the scene."

"I know," Micky said, giggling.

"All right, I'll go along with it," I said wearily. I had decided that I might as well cooperate because these three weren't going to let me do anything else. I shut my eyes and Sandy led me off to the left.

"Now open your eyes," she said.

I did, and I got the biggest shock of my life.

Chapter 2

There I was, in the student lounge, looking straight at *me*. Or rather, I was gawking at a girl who looked exactly like me. Same hair worn in the same style, same green eyes, same straight nose and slightly too short upper lip. She was wearing a duplicate of my pink sweater, and I had a hunch that when she stood up from the table, I'd see that she was wearing the identical gray skirt.

She touched her hair as if she were looking in a mirror and burst out laughing.

"Who are you?" she cried as she jumped up. I was wrong about the skirt. It was gray all right, but hers was pleated.

I turned to look at Micky and Sandy. "Now I'm the one who doesn't believe what I'm seeing."

Thad took the other girl by the shoulders. "Paige, this is your twin sister, Heather, who was separated from you at birth and taken away by a wicked witch."

"My mother is not a witch and I'm not a twin," I said. "But I can't believe that we aren't cousins at least."

"I don't have any cousins," she said, laughing. "I've

got two sisters, but they don't look much like me. I mean us." She looked around, then back at me. "We're collecting a crowd, Heather. Let's go somewhere private so we can talk."

I glanced around, too, and saw what she meant. A dozen students had dropped what they were doing and now openly stared at us. One of them, a boy almost as tall as Thad but with straight dark hair, grinned at me.

"I'm in heaven," he said. "Heather? Is that your name? Heather what? Where do you live?"

"Don't pay any attention to Colin," she said, but I could tell by the expression on her face that *she* wanted to pay a lot of attention to him. "Come on, Heather. Let's go find a quiet corner in the cafeteria and get acquainted."

I explained to Paige that I hadn't registered for classes yet. "I'd love to talk to you, though. Could we meet at lunch?"

Paige unfolded a sheet of paper. "I have second lunch this semester. See if you can get it, too. Take my schedule and ask for the same classes. We'll have fun."

"What about us?" Micky said. "Sandy and I found her first!"

"We'll *all* go to the office and sign her up," Paige said.

"Right," Thad said. "Everybody goes."

Colin took one of Paige's hands and one of mine. "I can't wait to see Mr. Stark's face when these two walk in."

"Who's Mr. Stark?" I asked as I was moved along by the crowd, out of the lounge and down the hall toward the office.

"The vice principal," Paige said. "He hates me. He'll hate you, too."

"He hates everybody," Sandy offered placidly.

"Except your stepsister and a couple of the other geniuses," Micky told me.

"If you're perfect, he likes you," Paige explained, "but if you're anything like me, he'll follow you around and watch every move you make."

"Wonderful," I said uneasily. "I can see that I'm going to be very happy here."

"Don't listen to Paige," Colin said, squeezing my hand. "She goes out of her way to hassle Mr. Stark."

"That's not true!" Paige exclaimed. But she was grinning.

They followed me through the office door. Tracey was still there, talking to a woman at the end of the counter. She looked up when I came in with my new friends.

"I can see that Micky and Sandy have been taking care of you," Tracey said. Then she noticed Paige and raised her eyebrows in astonishment. "I thought Heather looked familiar when I first saw her," she said, ignoring everybody when they began laughing. "You're Paige, the girl who won the talent show last year. I remember now. You're a good dancer."

My stepsister was one of the smartest people I'd ever met, but I was realizing just how absentminded she was, too.

A bell rang and my new friends left for their first classes. Tracey introduced me to the office clerk and left, too, while the clerk was arranging classes for me, using Paige's schedule as a guide. The only period we wouldn't be together was the one after second lunch. I had art then and Paige was taking a drama class.

"Your teachers won't be able to tell the two of you apart," Miss Cabrini said, grinning. "I hope you aren't as full of mischief as Paige."

"I can't promise," I said, and I grinned, too. Oh, fun, I thought. I wasn't going to miss my old school so much after all.

A door at the back of the office opened and a small, chubby man with a red face trotted out, glared at me, and hurried over to the counter where I was standing.

"You, Paige Worth," he said. "Why aren't you in class? What have you done now? This is only the first day of school and you've started in with your pranks already."

"I'm not Paige," I said. "I'm Heather Whitney."

"She's a new student," Miss Cabrini said quickly. "Heather Whitney from Seattle. She's Tracey Carver's stepsister. Heather, this is Mr. Stark, the vice principal."

Mr. Stark stared at me for a long moment. "Is this some sort of joke?"

I shook my head. "No."

"Did Paige put you up to this disguise?" he demanded, bouncing up and down on his toes. "I'm not going to tolerate any more of her nonsense. No more rubber chickens hanging in the cafeteria. No more car crash sound effects on the PA system when I'm reading the morning announcements. You had better understand me, Heather Whitney, because if you follow Paige's lead, you're going to find yourself in trouble with me, yes, indeed."

Rubber chickens? Car crash sound effects? Paige was going to be more fun than I'd even imagined.

Suddenly, stupidly, I burst out laughing. I don't know what was wrong with me. Nerves, maybe. Mr. Stark was so rude and so pompous, and I was more than slightly frazzled by the morning's events. I couldn't stop laughing, even when Miss Cabrini frowned and shook her head at me in warning.

"I fail to see the humor in this," Mr. Stark said. He puffed up his chest and his eyes goggled. "Education is a serious matter. Your stepsister realizes that and that is why she is such a successful student. You would do well to imitate her instead of Paige Worth."

I had lost my mind, obviously, because instead of sobering up, I only laughed harder. "Sorry," I sputtered. "I'm really sorry, but I can't help how I look."

He gave me one more withering scowl and then he turned and bounced away. His behind waggled like a fish tail.

I bit my lip until it hurt and did my best to stop laughing. "Have you finished with my schedule?" I asked the clerk.

She pushed it across the counter at me, and I could see that she was having trouble keeping her face sober. "This wasn't a good beginning, Heather," she said quietly. "Paige exasperates him deliberately. Your stepsister really is a better example."

But not half as much fun, I thought as I took my schedule and thanked her. I was still laughing when I reached my first class.

Paige sat in the back row, obviously waiting for me. The teacher looked up when I walked in, stared, and then grinned. "Not another one," he said. "I'm not sure I can take it."

"It must be something in the water in Fox Crossing," I said innocently as I showed him my schedule. "When I moved here, I was short and fat and I had curly red hair."

He scribbled his initials on my schedule. "Take a seat," he said, "as far away from your double as you can get."

As I walked away, I heard him mumble, "Must be something in the water." When I glanced back at him, I saw that he was laughing.

I loved it!

The loudspeaker on the wall crackled and everyone looked at it expectantly.

14

"Good morning," Mr. Stark's voice cried out of the speaker. "The faculty and student body of Fox Crossing High School welcome the incoming freshmen and the other new students. I'm certain that we'll all work together for the good of the school this year."

Paige snorted and rolled her eyes at me.

Mr. Stark coughed explosively into the mike and then went on, explaining student parking regulations, activity cards, and fire drills. No one seemed to be listening.

A short silence followed the announcements. Then I heard a sharp click and the soft hiss of a tape running.

"Now for the daily message from another planet," Paige whispered, grinning.

"Good morning, students," a squeaky and strained man's voice announced. "Here's a little thought for your day. No matter how easy life may seem to you at this moment, you may be sure . . . ah . . . that it will provide its challenges and rewards before the light fades in the west."

The class groaned in unison and then laughed. There was a light patter of applause.

"What was *that* all about?" I asked Paige.

"That's the principal, Mr. Zoppler. Every morning he gives us his thought for the day."

"But it didn't make very much sense," I said.

Paige giggled. "They never do. Do you know that I only saw him once all last year and that was when Miss Fisher, the old art teacher, had a nervous breakdown and threw a chair out her window? Mr. Zoppler left school early that day and I got a quick look at him running for his car. Most kids have never seen him at all."

"No wonder Mr. Stark is so nervous," I said.

"Oh, he'd be weird anyway," Paige assured me.

I ran into Tracey in the hall between classes and she asked me how I was getting along.

"I'm having a wonderful time," I told her.

"She's making lots of friends," Micky told her.

"Lots," Paige echoed.

"Good," Tracey said. "That's wonderful. If you have first lunch, you can come with me to the student lounge and play bridge if you like."

"I've got second lunch," I said, relieved. I had too much energy to sit around playing cards.

"Then I'll meet you by the front door after school and walk home with you," Tracey said.

"We're taking her out for hamburgers after school," Paige said. "Would you like to come with us, Tracey?"

Tracey shook her head. "Thank you very much. That's thoughtful of you, but I have lab experiments to plan." She smiled at me then and patted my arm. "You have a good time, though."

We watched her walk away, straight and tall and looking a little like a frumpy duchess.

"She does homework on the first day of school?" Paige asked.

"Yes, and that's why she won a four-year scholarship to college and you won't," Sandy said.

"I can't think that far ahead," Paige said. "Come on, let's go to class and scare the teacher into believing that she's got double vision."

I glanced back once as we ran off, wondering if Tracey felt left out, but I saw her standing with two other kids who looked like seniors, and I was certain that she'd forgotten about me.

At lunch break, Thad saved a whole table in the middle of the cafeteria, and he beckoned when he saw us come in, signaling that we were to sit with him.

I got in the food line with the others and told myself that Thad was only going to be a friend. But I couldn't help wishing that he was as interested in me as Colin seemed to be.

Or maybe Colin was interested in Paige. He'd called me by her name twice already that day.

He slid into line behind me. "Paige? Or are you Paige Two?"

"Quit that," I said, poking his arm. "If you think I'm going to put up with being called Paige Two, you're wrong."

"I'll quit," Colin said, and he leaned close to me. "I like saying your name, Heather. I plan on saying it a lot. Maybe I'll even carve it on a tree in front of the school."

"You will not," I said.

"In capital letters," he said.

"What are you two arguing about?" Paige said, turning around to grin at us.

"Change places with me," I told her. "I want to ask Micky something."

Paige would be glad to stand next to Colin—I could tell she liked him. I was new in school, and having a close girlfriend was important to me. I didn't want her to think that I might develop an interest in Colin. And I didn't want him to think that, either.

We switched places and Micky and I chose our lunches from a discouraging selection.

"The best time I ever had in here was the day Paige brought three ugly rubber chickens to school and wired them to that rack over the steam table," Micky said. "Everybody ordered rubber chicken instead of whatever awful stuff the cooks had fixed that day. Somebody tattled, though, and Mr. Stark came down and yelled so loud that the first lunch kids said you could hear him all over the school."

I grinned. "I already heard about the chickens from Mr. Stark. He seems to think I might do something just as bad."

"Is he right?" Micky asked hopefully.

17

I cocked my head to one side. "I'm considering the possibilities," I told her. "School food always offers so many interesting opportunities. Look at that rice, for instance. What are those little yellow balls in it?"

One of the servers leaned across the rice and glared. "I warned you last year not to start up with us again."

I blinked innocently. "Okay. I'll be good."

"But I won't promise anything," Paige said behind me.

The server looked at her, then back at me. "One was enough."

"Don't pay any attention to them," Colin said. "They're just looking like that to annoy everybody."

The server laughed in spite of herself. By the time Paige and I reached the table, we had the attention of everyone in the cafeteria.

"I'm not sure I can handle being stared at every day," I told her. "Let's check with each other so we don't wear the same things to school."

Paige shrugged. "Sure, if that makes you feel better. But I think you're missing the chance of a lifetime. Just think how crazy we can make Mr. Stark."

"You'll do that without wearing the same clothes," Thad said. "You're driving me crazy now." He wasn't smiling and I wondered if he was growing tired of the joke.

"Everybody will get used to us," I said quickly. "And Paige and I aren't exactly alike."

"You have a dimple and she doesn't," Thad said, looking closely at me.

He was blond, but he had black eyelashes. My heart thumped so loudly that I was afraid he could hear it, so I leaned away from him. "See how easy it will be to tell us apart?" I asked when I finally could talk again.

"I hope you're right," Colin said, intruding on a conversation that might have had incredible possibilities. "I

18

grew up with Paige, so I've heard all her jokes at least twice. I want to concentrate on you.''

Paige smiled when he said that, but I could read her mind. She didn't want Colin concentrating on anybody but her, but she was too nice to make a fuss.

"Believe me, my jokes are all so old they collect pensions," I told Colin, and then I turned my attention to Sandy, who was examining her bread with a scowl. "What's wrong with it?" I asked.

"This is exactly the same piece they gave me last spring," she said. "I recognize the hole in it. I wouldn't eat it then and I refuse to eat it now."

Everybody laughed and the awkward moment passed. I made up my mind then that I would go out of my way to avoid Colin. I didn't want to make any relationship mistakes.

After school, we went out for hamburgers, and I didn't get home until four-thirty. Tracey was studying in her bedroom and Mrs. Brier was in the kitchen, slamming pots and pans around.

"Where's Mom?" I asked her.

She looked up at me from under her heavy eyebrows. "She went off to that free medical clinic across town. She said that she was going to volunteer there." Her tone was so annoyed that I dropped the carrot I'd just picked up from the cutting board.

"Is there something wrong with that?"

"Dr. Carver's wife ought to do something more important," Mrs. Brier said. She moved the cutting board out of my reach.

It didn't take a genius to see that Mrs. Brier didn't like Mom or me, even though she hardly knew us. "Did Dr. Carver's first wife do something more important?" I blurted. "What exactly is more important in Fox Crossing?"

"Mind your manners," Mrs. Brier said coldly.

"I will if you mind yours," I snapped back furiously. "Mom has always volunteered to help out at free clinics. If you expect her to spend her time having lunch and going shopping, you'll be disappointed. Is that what Tracey's mother did?"

Mrs. Brier slammed a pan down on the stove. "No, and Tracey would have been better off if she had."

"What do you mean?" I asked.

"It's none of your business," she said. "Don't you have homework to do?" She went into the pantry and slammed the door behind her.

Wow, I thought. I knew that Dr. Carver and his wife had been divorced for a long time. Whatever could the first Mrs. Carver have done to make Mrs. Brier hate her so much? Did Mom realize that Mrs. Brier didn't like her either? I needed a chance to talk to her privately.

But Mom came home with Will just before dinner was served, so I didn't get a chance to tell her anything.

After dinner we had dessert in the den again, and Will put on another symphony and played an elaborate word game with Mom and Tracey. I begged off and went upstairs to my room to watch my small television. Before I went to bed, I wrote a letter to Amelia, telling her about my first day at school and Paige. I knew she'd laugh at that.

"There's a mystery here at home," I added. "The housekeeper doesn't like us, and she didn't like Tracey's mother, either. I wonder why."

I thought about telling her that I was a little disappointed about the Carvers because they were so quiet and, well, dull, but then I decided that I'd better not. After all, I'd only been in their house for a day. Maybe they'd liven up a little after I got to know them.

At least I hoped so. I didn't know how much of this word-game-and-symphony stuff I could take.

I didn't know how much of Mrs. Brier I could take, either.

I consoled myself with my favorite fantasy—I'd come home from school to a big, comfortable house and see my little brother and sister playing with a dog and cat. My mom would be slicing freshly baked bread and my stepfather would be setting the table for dinner. And everybody would be glad to see me and say so out loud.

In the fantasy, my stepfather did absolutely awful card tricks, like Uncle Jock, and laughed at himself when the cards shot all over the room. And he watched football on TV with a cat asleep in his lap. He fixed things around the house and complained about his car. And he told me over and over that I was just as pretty as my mother.

I knew my daydream needed some updating, but I liked it the way it was. After all, I'd been working on it for years.

Chapter 3

Thought for the day: Each of us should spend time every day wondering what other people think of us. This teaches us humility.

Harold Z. Zoppler, Principal
Fox Crossing High School

Paige called me every morning before school to check on what I was wearing. Sometimes we made certain that we'd look completely different. Sometimes we couldn't resist seeing how far we could push our amazing resemblance. The kids at school enjoyed this, and the attention I got took my mind off the Carver house. I owed Paige a lot for befriending me so enthusiastically.

The first time Mom saw Paige she nearly fainted. She had started her volunteer work at the clinic right away so one afternoon Paige and I found the clinic and went in.

The reception room was jammed with people. Mom was standing near the counter, talking to a woman with a sick baby. But the patients saw us, and everybody stopped talking at the same moment.

Mom looked up when she noticed the silence. She saw us and gasped. "Heather?" she asked, looking first at me and then at Paige.

"Heather!" she repeated, staring straight at me. "For heaven's sake!"

"This is Paige, Mom. Remember, I told you there was a girl at school who looked like me."

22

"I know you said that, Heather," Mom said, "but I didn't think you meant she looked almost exactly like you."

A buzz of conversation began in the reception room, and one child started crying.

"Are we scaring him?" Paige asked.

"You scared me for a moment," Mom said, and she laughed. "There has to be a logical explanation for this. Paige, are you certain you don't have Whitney relatives?"

"I'm absolutely sure," Paige told her. "My mother has traced our family tree back four generations, and there's not a Whitney perched on a branch anywhere. Everybody's supposed to have a double, and Heather and I are lucky we found each other."

"Hmm," Mom said. "I'll bet the school doesn't think this was such a lucky break."

"Why, Mom," I said innocently, "you don't think I'd take advantage of this, do you?"

"I know that you would—in a minute!" Mom said. "Come for dinner tonight, Paige. I want Will to see this. But the two of you must behave yourselves. Mrs. Brier won't think this is funny."

She shouldn't have reminded me of the housekeeper, because I can't resist temptation. By the time Paige and I got home, we'd worked out a prank to make Mrs. Brier laugh, if anything could.

Paige ran into the kitchen first, and Mrs. Brier looked up. "I hope you wiped your feet," she said. She stirred something in a pot on the stove and barely glanced at Paige.

"My shoes are clean," Paige said soberly.

"Then you can make yourself useful. I did the wash today, and the towels for your bathroom are folded up in the laundry room. You'll have to put them away yourself. I'm not here to wait on you."

Paige shot a quick look at me, standing in the doorway. "I don't know where the laundry room is," she said to Mrs. Brier.

Mrs. Brier glared at Paige. "You've got a short memory," she said, "since you're the one who left the door open yesterday."

"I don't remember doing that, but I bet Heather does," Paige said, and she burst out laughing.

I stepped into the kitchen, but I was already regretting this idea. Mrs. Brier didn't look surprised, only annoyed.

"I don't have time for your childish pranks, missy," she said to me, and she turned back to the stove as if nothing out of the ordinary had happened.

Chagrined, Paige and I crept away.

"She really is a grouch," Paige said as we reached my room.

"Is there something worse than just a grouch?" I asked. "That doesn't describe her. I've been here for days and she hasn't smiled at me once."

Paige bounced on the bed, then leaned back against my pillows. "Does Mrs. Brier smile at Tracey?"

"Sure," I said. I sat down at my desk, pulled a bag of chocolates out of a drawer, and passed it to Paige. "She's crazy about Tracey and Will."

"Are you jealous?" Paige asked sympathetically.

I shook my head. "No, of course not. They're both terrific people. And Mrs. Brier's been here since Tracey's mother left ten years ago, so naturally she prefers Tracey to me. But gee, I wish she weren't so rude. It's depressing."

Paige swallowed one chocolate and took another. "Can't you make her laugh? Cheer her up?"

"Nothing works. She acts as if I were a criminal."

"I suppose you have to look on the good side," Paige

24

said. "At least you don't have to do a lot of chores around here. I wish we had a housekeeper."

"I don't mind housework. In fact, I wish Mrs. Brier weren't here. I had lots of fun at Amelia's, helping out."

"You," Paige said, "are crazy. I'm so tired of picking up after my sisters that sometimes I'd like to drag them to the pound and see if I could trade them in for two more dogs."

I grinned. Paige's family already had three dogs. "You don't need any more pets, but I wish I had one. I'm going to ask Will if we can get a dog. Tracey used to have one but it got old and died, and since she's going away to college next year, they decided not to get another one."

"Thad's father found two abandoned puppies a few weeks ago," Paige said, sitting up. "They're keeping one, but I bet he'd give you the other. They're really cute."

I heard the front door close downstairs. "That's probably Tracey. She was going to the library after school. Let's ask her what she thinks about getting a puppy."

I invited Tracey in to share chocolates with us, and she thought the puppy was a good idea. When Will came home, he agreed, too. Over dinner, Mom also said she thought a puppy would be fun.

But Mrs. Brier, holding a platter of meat so that Tracey could choose a piece, said, "There won't be any puppies in this house."

Mom, Paige, and I exchanged quick looks.

"A puppy might be nice for Heather," Will said. He smiled at Mrs. Brier. "I'm sure she'll take care of it herself."

"Who's going to take care of it when she's in school and when she's running around with her friends?" Mrs. Brier grumbled. She thrust the platter at Mom as if she hoped some of the meat would fall off in Mom's lap.

25

Mom seemed to take her lead from Will. She calmly helped herself and then said, "I'm only spending half the day at the clinic. I'll watch the pup in the mornings. You'll only have to keep an eye on it until Heather gets home from school."

Mrs. Brier's face flushed an ugly dark red. She slammed the platter down on the table in front of Paige and left the room.

No one said anything for a long, long minute. Then Will cleared his throat and said cheerfully, "Heather, I think we should drive over to the Shiptons' house this evening and talk to them about a puppy."

"Will, are you sure?" Mom asked, almost in a whisper. "If this is going to be a problem . . ."

"It won't be a problem," Tracey said. "I'll be glad to have a dog in the house again. And you'll be here to love it when I'm gone next year, Heather."

Tracey and Will acted as if Mrs. Brier hadn't been rude. Maybe they were used to her, but I wasn't. And Paige had been awfully silent since the meat landed in front of her.

"I'm sorry, Paige. You must wish you hadn't stayed for dinner," I said.

She shrugged, but she didn't look up from her plate.

"Mrs. Brier is sometimes thoughtless," Will said. "I hope you won't take her seriously, Paige."

"How can she help it?" I blurted. "I take Mrs. Brier seriously, too. She's always angry. I know she doesn't like me, and she treats—"

"Heather," Mom said warningly, "I don't think we need to inflict our family discussions on Paige."

"Oh, that's all right," Paige said, looking up from her plate. She was grinning. "It sounds like home. Except that we usually discuss things at the top of our lungs and make the dogs bark."

Paige and I laughed, and Mom grinned in spite of

herself. But Will and Tracey simply looked at us politely, as if Paige had commented on the weather. Or as if they were too kind to acknowledge that Paige had just admitted that her family quarreled.

Paige blushed.

As soon as we could, we excused ourselves from the table. I explained that I was going to walk Paige home, and both of us fled from the house.

"Did I ever feel stupid," Paige said when we were half a block away. "Your stepfather doesn't have a sense of humor, does he?"

"Not much. He's nice, but I don't think he knows what's funny." I stuck my hands in my pockets and sighed.

"Mrs. Brier reminds me of a vampire."

"She's not even that nice," I said. "Think of something worse."

Paige snickered. "She's the monster that hides in the closet and scares you to death when you're five years old."

I felt a lot better. By the time we reached Paige's house, Mrs. Brier didn't seem so awful anymore.

Paige's parents welcomed me enthusiastically, after they got over their surprise. The Worth family reminded me of Amelia's. Her parents were good-natured and casual, Paige's younger sisters were as sweet as my little cousins, and the dogs were great.

Mr. Paige had brought home two cartoon videotapes for Paige's sisters. Paige's music was playing on the stereo in the family room. I couldn't help but wish that they'd invite me over for an evening soon. I had a hunch the Worths didn't play word games or listen to symphonies every night. And the house wasn't so quiet that you could hear every clock tick. I was sorry to leave.

When I was halfway home, a car stopped next to me and Colin yelled, "Hey, Paige, where are you going?"

"To Heather's," I said, hiding my grin.

"I'll give you a ride," he called out, so I climbed in the car beside him. "I've had my driver's license for two weeks and you're the first girl I've taken anywhere."

"Congratulations," I said.

"You're not Paige," he accused. "That's not her jacket."

"You're catching on," I told him. "Darn it. I was hoping I could fool you forever."

"You took me by surprise," he said. "Where's your house? I'll need to know that for future reference."

I directed him to the Carver house and asked him if he wanted to come inside for a while. "We're going to call Thad to see if he'll give us one of his puppies. Would you like to go?"

It didn't take any persuasion. He called Thad for me, thank goodness, because I didn't know Thad very well. Everybody except Mrs. Brier rode in the station wagon to the Shiptons, and half an hour later we brought a puppy home. Thad followed us in his car with the dog's toys, her bed, and half a ton of puppy kibble.

I named her Bear. We thought she might be half German shepherd and half Saint Bernard, but we couldn't be sure. She looked like she was wearing somebody else's big black and tan coat, but she was all wrinkly and so absolutely adorable that we argued over who was going to hold her on the way home. I won because I refused to let go of her. Bear must have liked that, because she wagged her tail as she gnawed off one of my jacket buttons.

Thad came in with us to supervise everything. Mom wanted to put Bear's bed in the back hall, but Thad said the pup should be in my room. Mrs. Brier scowled.

Will thought Bear should eat in the kitchen, but Mrs. Brier objected immediately, so Thad suggested that the pup eat in the laundry room. Mrs. Brier hated that idea, too. Will patted the pup and said she'd eat in the kitchen, just the way the old dog had. Mrs. Brier folded her lips together in a hard line, but she didn't argue anymore.

Thad and Colin put Bear's toys on the den floor, and Bear settled right down to chew on a nylon bone.

"We're going to miss her," Thad said. He had such a sad look on his face that I wanted to hug him.

"You can come to visit her," I said.

"Sure, we'll come over to see her often," Colin said. Thad didn't say anything.

Mrs. Brier left the room and slammed the door behind her.

"She doesn't like dogs, does she?" Thad asked uneasily. "Maybe Bear shouldn't stay here."

"Bear's going to be fine," I said.

"Believe me, there won't be a problem," Tracey said. She rubbed Bear's ears.

"No, there won't," Will said. "Excuse me a moment." He left the room and closed the door.

I looked at Tracey and she met my gaze firmly. "Dad will straighten it out, Heather."

But I had an awful feeling in the pit of my stomach.

Thad and Colin left together. As he went to the door, I hoped that Thad would say he'd call to see how the pup and I were getting along. Instead, he said, "I hope you'll tell me if it turns out that the puppy isn't welcome here, Heather."

I was chilled by his tone, but I understood his concern. "I love her and I'm going to see that she's all right, Thad," I said. "Mrs. Brier is just cranky because of me. It doesn't have anything to do with Bear."

But I could tell that he wasn't convinced when he left.

I carried Bear upstairs, and Tracey followed us. "Mrs. Brier takes understanding, Heather. Bear's going to be happy here."

"Your dad doesn't think so," I said, struggling to control my anger. "That's why he's in the kitchen talking to Mrs. Brier."

Tracey blinked. "I suppose he's talking about her attitude. But you can't believe that Dad would let her stay here if she was capable of hurting a puppy."

I hugged Bear to my chest so hard that she grunted. "No, I guess not."

But I wrote to Amelia again that night, telling her that I wasn't sure if Bear was safe with the old witch of a housekeeper. I promised myself that I'd run all the way home from school every day until I could trust Mrs. Brier. If ever.

In the morning, Mrs. Brier was polite to both Mom and me, for a change. She even bent down and patted Bear. But her eyes were cold and mean, and when I left for school, I felt like crying. I looked back at the big house and wished with all my heart that I could take Bear and go to Seattle. This wasn't the family I'd daydreamed about all my life. This was awful.

Tracey didn't notice my mood. She talked all the way to school about her college plans, but I only half listened. We were about half a block from school when something odd happened.

Two kids were standing on the sidewalk talking. The boy was short and freckled, with a mouth that turned down on one side in a natural sneer. The girl was overweight and scowling.

"Good morning, Darren, Kix," Tracey said as we passed. Her voice sounded a little strained. They didn't answer, and when we were a couple of steps away, the boy whispered something and both of them laughed nastily. Their hostility was chilling.

"Who are they?" I asked.

"A couple of the seniors," Tracey said. "Guess I should have introduced you to them."

"I can live without knowing them," I said.

Tracey sighed. "So could I."

"What's going on between the three of you?"

She shrugged. "Nothing, really. We just have different opinions on things."

"Like what?" I urged.

"Believe me, it doesn't matter," Tracey said. "You wouldn't be the least bit interested. Hey, there's Micky and Sandy. You'll have to tell them about Bear."

Then, before I could protest, Tracey hurried away from me and went up the school steps with one of her friends.

Now what was that all about? I wondered. But then I caught up with Micky and Sandy and started talking about my new puppy, so I didn't think about Darren and Kix again for a long time.

Paige was waiting inside the door for us. She was wearing big glasses with a plastic nose and a black moustache attached. "I thought I'd make it easy for everybody today," she said soberly.

"You, new girl—Heather, is it?—take that ridiculous thing off right now!"

Mr. Stark toddled toward us. "I warned you about disrupting the school," he cried. "Take that off!"

"Okay," I said. I reached out and pulled the glasses off Paige.

Underneath the false moustache, she had drawn another on her upper lip with eyeliner. Solemnly, she took a card out of her purse and pinned it to her sweater. It read, "Paige Worth, an original."

"Good morning, Mr. Stark," she said sweetly, and she twitched her upper lip so that her moustache wiggled.

Amelia would have cracked up over that.

Chapter 4

Thought for the day: Enjoy life while you're young, if you can, because it only gets worse.

Harold Z. Zoppler, Principal
Fox Crossing High School

After my last class, I ran straight home from school with some of my new friends for moral support. I was worried about Bear—and so was Thad. He didn't say much, but he'd lost his sense of humor. He'd even stopped teasing me about my resemblance to Paige. When I invited him to visit the puppy, he accepted so quickly that I felt a little angry. The puppy was more important to him than I was. Well, why not? Bear was a defenseless baby, and I could stand up for myself around Mrs. Brier.

As soon as I opened the front door, I heard Bear whining. Mrs. Brier had shut her up in the basement in the dark! We found poor Bear huddled in her bed, trembling. I grabbed her and hugged her.

"At least she's got food and water," Thad said. He looked around the basement uneasily. "This isn't a good place for a dog, Heather. I think I'd better take Bear home with me."

"It's an awful place," I said. "And Bear isn't going to stay in it again." I stomped up the steps, with Paige right behind me, followed by Micky and Sandy, Thad and Colin. We made quite an army. I hoped that we'd intimidate Mrs. Brier.

I marched into the kitchen. Mrs. Brier sat at the table, reading. She looked up from her magazine, stared at Bear, and then looked back down again, ignoring the rest of us.

"You were supposed to take care of the puppy until I got home," I said angrily.

"It wet on the hall carpet," she said, smirking. "Dr. Carver isn't going to like that when I tell him about it."

I blew up. "He's going to hate hearing that you shut Bear up in the basement," I said. "I'm going to call him right now." I was so upset that I was shaking all over.

"You can't interrupt him when he's at the college. No one does that, not even his *own* daughter." Mrs. Brier looked around at my friends. "They have to leave, Heather. You don't have permission to bring guests here after school."

She scared me, but I wasn't going to let her know it. "Will didn't say that I needed permission to invite friends to my house."

Mrs. Brier lifted her lip scornfully. *"Your* house?"

I stalked out of the kitchen with the kids trailing behind.

"Look, Heather, just let me take the puppy back," Thad said earnestly. "Bear's only going to make trouble for you."

I walked straight to the hall table where the phone sat, and holding Bear with one arm, I paged through the phone book until I found the number of the college.

"Are you sure you should call your stepfather?" Paige asked. "What if he gets mad?"

"He won't," I said, but I wasn't certain. "He spoke to Mrs. Brier about her attitude last night. I guess it didn't do any good. Now I'm going to tell him what she did to the puppy."

Will was in his office, so I was speaking to him before

I had planned what to say, and I ended up babbling, and finally crying.

Calmly, Will said, "Call Mrs. Brier to the phone, Heather. Don't be upset. I'm certain that she misunderstood. You bring Bear's things back upstairs, and that's where they'll stay."

I went to the kitchen to tell Mrs. Brier that Dr. Carver wanted to talk to her. She didn't say anything to me, but I knew from her expression that the war wasn't over.

After we brought up the puppy's things, my friends gathered in the den with me, and I held Bear close in my arms.

"This won't work," Thad said. "Please let me take Bear back."

"That might be a good idea, Heather," Paige said.

"No, it's not," Micky said. "She can't let Mrs. Brier treat her like this. Dr. Carver's on Heather's side, and he's Mrs. Brier's boss. That has to count for something."

"But the puppy's caught in the middle," Thad said.

Tracey came in then, and Sandy told her what had happened. Tracey's mouth tightened, but she didn't raise her voice when she said, "Don't worry about it. Dad and I will handle this."

How could she and Will stay so calm? They never seemed to get upset about anything. I was half crazy with worry, and I had a headache that went clear to my ankles.

When Mrs. Brier hung up the phone, Tracey went out to talk to her, and we listened without bothering to hide our curiosity.

"I want to keep this puppy, Mrs. Brier," Tracey said flatly. "I miss having a dog. Don't shut her in the basement again."

"No one told me not to put the pup in the basement,"

Mrs. Brier argued. "Anyway, I thought you didn't want another dog."

"We have one now, Heather and I. I'm going to talk to Dad about this, just to make certain of what he told you. And I want him to know what I told you. That way there won't be any confusion about how you're supposed to treat the puppy."

"Before *they* came here . . ." Mrs. Brier began.

"Shall I tell Dad that you're unhappy here?" Tracey asked.

After a moment, Mrs. Brier said, "Never mind."

Paige and I exchanged a triumphant look. We could hear Mrs. Brier's shoes clop off to the kitchen, and she banged a couple of pans around so we'd know she wasn't permanently defeated.

Tracey looked in. "I'm going to the library," she said, as if nothing had happened. "Can I pick up something for you, Heather?"

"No, thanks," I told her. After she left, everybody else took off, too, except Thad.

"You can come over anytime you like to check on Bear," I told him. "But I'm sure everything will be fine. You can see that my family really wants a dog."

"Sure," he said doubtfully. "Maybe I'll help you train Bear on a leash. She's old enough to start learning a few things. She'll be more popular if she's trained."

"You can housebreak her for me," I said, grinning, trying to cheer things up.

He grinned a little, too. "No, thanks. I've got my hands full with my own puppy."

"I'll bet housebreaking's the hard part," I said. We were at the front door then, and Bear had fallen asleep in my arms. She was awfully heavy to carry around for so long.

"You're right," Thad said. He scratched Bear's ear, smiled when she grunted a little puppy protest, and then he walked out on the porch. "If there's a problem, will you call me?" he asked.

I nodded. As he left, he looked back once, and I suspected that he didn't like me much. Oh, it was fun at first to joke about how much I looked like Paige, but now something serious had happened regarding Bear, and he didn't feel like laughing about anything. I was new in school, and right away I'd introduced a problem into his life. That wasn't a good start.

I went inside and shut the door. Mrs. Brier was standing only a few feet away. "You think you're smart, don't you?" she said.

I brushed past her on my way to the stairs. I wasn't going to let her goad me, but my stomach felt as if it were full of nails.

"I'm not going to make your bed or clean up your room," she said tauntingly as I climbed the stairs.

"I didn't ask you to," I said. "I only want you to make sure Bear is all right from the time Mom leaves at one o'clock until I come home at three." I glared over the banister at her. "Mom and Tracey and I will do everything else."

"You bet you will," she said, smiling the nastiest smile I'd ever seen.

I hated her! I never hated anybody so much in my entire life! Upstairs I slammed my bedroom door so hard that I woke up Bear.

After she went back to sleep again, this time on my bed, I wrote a long letter to Amelia, telling her exactly how awful Mrs. Brier was. And how wonderful it was to have my own puppy. When I finished the letter, I felt a lot better. It took all my willpower not to add a line saying that I wanted to return to Seattle. I had a family now, and one way or another, I was going to be happy here.

But that was easier to say than to do. After dinner,

Mom and Will sat in the den again, listening to music and reading. Tracey played with Bear for a while, then went upstairs to start her homework. Bear fell asleep before I had a chance to play with her, so I had my choice of sitting in the den listening to music that made me yawn or starting my own homework. I didn't want to do either. I was still upset because of Mrs. Brier, and I desperately needed something to distract me.

"Do you ever watch TV?" I asked Will.

He looked up from his book and considered my question. "There was a series that I enjoyed very much last spring," he said.

Mom grinned at me. "You can watch if you like, Heather, as long as your homework is finished."

I didn't really want to watch TV. I wanted conversation, about anything at all. "What are you reading, Will?" I asked.

He looked up again. Patiently. "This is a mystery novel," he said. "I'm very fond of mysteries. Do you like them, Heather?"

"Not much," I said.

"Ah," he said. He'd forgotten me already.

"Oh, for heaven's sake, Heather," Mom said ruefully. "Will's going to think that you can't entertain yourself."

"Of course I can," I said. I got up and left Bear sleeping on the rug. I could hear Tracey's radio playing faintly, and I hoped I'd find her door open when I got upstairs, but it was closed. I had a hunch that if I knocked, she'd be polite. And very patient with me until she could get rid of me.

I went to my room and read the short story I'd been assigned in English that day. I loved it, but when I went downstairs to tell Mom about it, she and Will were playing a card game, so I didn't interrupt. Mrs. Brier had

37

gone home, not that I would have tried to discuss anything with her. I called Paige instead.

I ended up feeling worse. In the background, I heard her sisters laughing, and the deep, friendly rumble of her dad's voice. My cousin's house sounded that way. But not mine. Never mine.

The next day, Friday, Thad went home from school with me again, to help me take Bear out on a leash. Bear's antics had us laughing before we'd gone a block. She insisted on holding part of the leash in her mouth, as if she were leading herself. She certainly didn't follow my directions.

"How big do you suppose she's going to get?" I asked.

Thad eyed Bear speculatively. "She's going to be huge. Look at her feet."

The weather was cool for September, and my jacket wasn't heavy enough to keep out the wind that was blowing the first autumn leaves from the birch trees. "I'll be glad when Bear can walk a little faster," I said. "I wish my coat were as heavy as hers."

"Let's cut through the park," Thad said. "We'll get back to your place sooner that way."

Bear enjoyed the park—it was impossible to keep her on the path. She'd have cheerfully strangled herself before obeying.

"I don't think this training is working," I told Thad.

"Give her a chance," he said. "She's still a baby."

I hauled Bear back on the path for the millionth time, while Thad watched. "I think she slept the whole time after Mom left this afternoon," I told him. "Now she's full of energy."

"I'm glad she slept," he said. "At least—"

"I know. At least she didn't have to put up with Mrs. Brier. But I don't think there's going to be a problem anymore. I wish we didn't have a housekeeper. Mom and I could do everything."

Thad lifted Bear up on the curb. "Do you miss Seattle?"

"Yes," I admitted.

"I suppose you had lots of friends there."

"Sure. But I'm making friends here, too."

"Did you have a boyfriend?" he asked. He pulled Bear away from too close an inspection of a plastic bag in the gutter.

I shrugged. "Not exactly."

He looked at me sideways. "Colin likes you."

"Colin can't tell me apart from Paige," I said, laughing.

"Neither can I, sometimes," Thad said. He took a piece of paper away from Bear. "You don't have any brothers or sisters?"

"I have Tracey now." He was asking a lot of questions.

"Where's your real dad?"

"He died when I was a baby," I said. I know I sounded a bit unfriendly, but I couldn't tell if he was asking me all those questions because he was interested in me or because he was still checking me out as Bear's new owner.

"It must be tough, growing up without a father."

"I have a cousin who's worse off," I said. "Erin's parents were killed in a car accident and she lives with her grandparents in Oregon now."

"That's awful," Thad said, and he sounded genuinely sorry. "Do you see her very often?"

"Not since she moved to Oregon. She doesn't even answer my letters. But I see my cousin Amelia all the time. Well, I did. She was my best friend in Seattle."

"Maybe you can go back to visit," he said, but I suspected that he didn't much care whether I did or not.

Rain began falling, big drops that rattled in the leaves of the trees we passed. "I wish I'd never left Seattle," I blurted.

"You mean that?" he asked. He picked up Bear and held her under his jacket so she wouldn't get wet.

"Yes. Well, sometimes." We'd reached my house and I should have asked him in, but I didn't. "Thanks for the help with Bear," I told him as I opened the door.

"We can do it again," he said, but I didn't give him a chance to say anything more.

"Good-bye," I said, and I took Bear from him and shut the door.

Mrs. Brier was waiting. "Wipe your feet," she snapped.

I kicked off my shoes and picked them up. "My socks aren't wet," I grumbled. I carried Bear upstairs and didn't look back.

Tracey stuck her head out her door. "I heard you took Bear out for a lesson on her leash. How'd it go?"

"Not too well," I said. "She has a mind of her own."

"Sorry about that," she said politely. I could tell that she wasn't interested in any details. "Mom and Will are going out tonight. If you want to make some plans, I'll watch Bear for you."

"Don't you and John go out on Fridays?"

"Usually," she said, "but he's got a cold so he's staying in tonight. Why don't you and your friends go to a movie?"

That wasn't a bad idea, so I called Paige and asked her. In half an hour, we'd gathered together a crowd of kids, including Colin. Paige had called Thad, but he wasn't home. That was all right. He'd probably had enough of me for one day.

Mom and Will hadn't left yet when the kids arrived to pick me up. Colin honked his horn half a dozen times, causing Mrs. Brier to lose her temper in the kitchen. She made more noise banging pans than Colin did with his horn.

Micky and Sandy came in to get me. "Look what we've got," Micky said, and she thrust a paper bag at me. "It's for Mrs. Brier. You can surprise her with it if you want."

"It's a little early for Halloween but we thought she'd appreciate it," Sandy said.

I reached into the bag and pulled out a dog mask. It looked like Bear was probably going to look someday, only meaner. "You think Mrs. Brier will wear this on Halloween?" I asked. "No way."

"It's for you to wear," Sandy said. "Here. Put it on and then go find her. I bet it makes her laugh."

"Never," I said. "I'm afraid of what she'll do to me."

Paige came in then, demanding to know why we were holding everybody up. "Haven't you tried out that mask on Mrs. Brier yet?" she asked. "Give it to me. Is she in the kitchen?"

"She's cleaning up the dinner dishes," I said, "and I'm sure she's in a bad mood. I wouldn't go in if I were you."

But Paige put on the mask and ran down the hall to the kitchen. "Mrs. Brier, can I have something to eat?" she cried as she shoved open the kitchen door.

Mrs. Brier let out a yell you could hear for a mile. "You terrible girl! You could have frightened me into a heart attack!"

Mom and Will rushed downstairs. "What's going on?" Mom demanded.

"It was only a joke," I said weakly.

Mrs. Brier came out of the kitchen clutching the mask. When she saw me, she stopped, but only for a second. "My nerves can't take these tricks, Dr. Carver," she cried. "Look at this mask!"

41

Will looked soberly from Paige to me. He took the mask, examined it, and then handed it back to Paige. "I can see that it might startle someone. But there's no real harm done."

Mrs. Brier turned abruptly and went back to the kitchen.

"I'll bet she bangs a pan," I said as I hunched my shoulders.

A pan banged in the kitchen.

Will didn't crack even a hint of a smile. "I believe someone's honking for you, girls," he said.

Mom was scowling, however. "For heaven's sake, tell that boy to quit all the racket, Heather. Aren't you leaving now?"

I nodded and ran for the front door. There had never been a joke that fell flatter than my last one.

But Uncle Jock would have laughed.

The next morning, Paige and I took Bear for a walk. The sky was bright blue, but a cold wind was blowing again. "The weather is different in Fox Crossing," I said.

"Sure," Paige said. "That's because we're so close to the mountains. We have more snow, too. You'll love it."

I wasn't too sure. I'd always believed that snow belonged on Christmas cards. But it was easy to tell that the puppy was going to like snow—she was absolutely crazy about mud and water.

"Did you and Colin go straight home after you dropped me off last night?" I asked. Colin had said he was hungry after we left the movie, but no one else was and so we didn't stop anywhere.

"We had pizza at that place across from the mall," she said. "I wish you'd come," she added.

I studied her face and said, "No, you don't," and I laughed.

"Have you been reading my mind?" she demanded, blushing.

"It's not exactly a hard thing to do since you turn red and start giggling every time you see him."

"I do not turn red!" she cried, and then she stopped in her tracks. "How awful. He must think I'm a complete idiot."

"I was only teasing. Probably he doesn't even notice that you blush—I don't think boys notice things like that. Has he ever taken you out?"

"Not on a real date, but we all go to movies together. I keep hoping he'll ask me to a dance, but he doesn't."

"He doesn't like anybody else better," I said firmly.

But I felt uncomfortable then, remembering how Colin was behaving toward me. No, I thought, I'm wrong. He's only being nice to a new girl in school. I wished that Thad would try it.

Bear grew so quickly that I could see a change in her nearly every day when I got home. Twice a week Thad came by to give her lessons on a leash. He concentrated on the puppy, not on me. But he asked me lots of questions about Mrs. Brier every time. Was she being kind to the pup? Was she keeping her out of the basement? I told him that Bear slept in my room every afternoon from the time Mom left until I got home, but Thad wasn't reassured.

It was impossible for me to like Mrs. Brier, and she knew it. I was sure that she enjoyed saying and doing things that made me uncomfortable. However, I wouldn't tattle on her again unless she did something to Bear.

Once, when Mom and I were in the house alone, I asked her about Tracey's mother.

Mom shrugged. "I only know she's never tried to

43

contact Will or Tracey since she left for New York. She wanted to make a career for herself in the theater.''

"Mrs. Brier thinks you should be satisfied shopping and having lunch with your friends instead of volunteering at the clinic.''

Mom laughed. "That sounds too much like waiting around to die,'' she said.

"Doesn't Mrs. Brier make you mad? How can you stand being here with her every morning?''

"She doesn't bother me now. We have an arrangement.''

"Like what? I'd like to have the same arrangement. Did you threaten her with one of her pans?''

Mom grinned. "No, I told her that I was here to stay so she had better pretend that she liked the idea.'' Mom sobered suddenly. "You haven't complained, so I thought you were managing, too.''

I shrugged. "I can live with things, as long as she's good to the puppy.''

I didn't add that Mrs. Brier wasn't the only one in the house who made me uneasy. Will and Tracey were always kind and never criticized me. But I felt like a guest who didn't interest them very much. They tried too hard to be good to me. There was no give and take, no joking around. I'd have appreciated an argument, if I'd thought that they cared about me one way or another.

I was lonely. The evenings stretched out forever, unless my friends came over or I went to someone else's house. I loved visiting Paige because her house reminded me of Amelia's. It was noisy and full of laughter and arguments. The rooms were cluttered with books and hobby materials. The dogs barked and the phone rang and everybody was alive!

At the big, perfect Carver house, the family was quiet and polite—and unemotional. And the clocks ticked and ticked in the long silences. I wanted to go home to Seattle.

I dreamed about Amelia's house so often that I was beginning to look forward to bedtime. Sometimes my dreams about my cousin's family were so vivid that I'd wake up in the morning thinking I was still there. And when I realized that I wasn't, I had a hard time not crying.

Chapter 5

During the next month Bear learned to walk on a leash, and she quit leaving puddles on the carpets. She also grew larger. And then she grew some more just in case we didn't think she was big enough. She chewed up one of my sneakers, both of Tracey's slippers, Will's favorite wool hat from England, Mom's new purse—and one of Mrs. Brier's wooden spoons. Everybody except Mrs. Brier forgave Bear because she was teething. Mrs. Brier never forgave anybody for anything.

The weather changed and grew colder. By early October, there was frost on the lawn in the mornings. Leaves fell, along with floods of cold rain.

Tracey and I came close to running out of things to talk about on the way to school in the mornings. She would have been content to walk in silence, but I kept trying to make conversation. Sometimes I got pretty desperate.

"How did you win the college scholarship?" I asked her one Monday when we were halfway to school.

"When I was a junior, Mr. Stark told us about a scholarship being offered by an archaeological society, so I wrote an essay and entered it. I never dreamed I'd win." She grinned and looked a whole lot prettier. "It was the most exciting thing that ever happened to me. The scholarship will be officially awarded to me at the honors assembly in February."

"I thought you already had it. That's what everybody says."

"Oh, I've got it. Mr. Stark told me last June, before school let out for the summer. But someone from the scholarship committee will come in February and award it to me during the ceremony. Sometimes I think I've only dreamed this." Her eyes were shining while she talked, and her voice had a lilt to it that I'd never heard before.

"What was the essay about?" I asked.

"Clothes," she said.

I gawked at her. "You wrote an essay about clothes for an archaeological society? Oh, I see. You wrote about the clothes people wore a long time ago."

"And then I compared them with what people will probably be wearing in the future. It seemed to me that some of the ways people dressed a couple of thousand years ago made more sense than the way we dress now, but I think that we'll come to our senses in the future and go back to simple clothes again."

I considered that. "Sounds good to me," I said. "We wouldn't have to struggle in and out of pantyhose anymore."

Tracey laughed out loud. That was the first time I'd ever heard her do that.

"Your essay sounds interesting," I told her, and I really meant it. "I'd love to read it—if you'd let me."

She actually blushed. "I'll give you a copy when we get home today."

"I thought archaeologists only cared about old temples and tombs."

"I'm more interested in the artifacts of ancient fami-

47

lies," she said. "I want to learn about their households and their personal belongings—oh, just everything that has to do with family living."

I didn't say anything, but I was thinking all sorts of things. Tracey didn't know very much about modern families; the Carver household was too formal and too quiet to count as an actual family, at least in my opinion. We were more like actors in a dull play, speaking lines that we had memorized. Everything was so—*controlled*. Maybe Tracey didn't realize what she was missing, and so she was searching for it in history. It occurred to me that in her own way, Tracey was as lonely as I, but she didn't know it.

Paige was waiting by my locker for me. We were wearing red sweaters that day, but they weren't identical. While I was hanging up my jacket, Colin trotted past. "Have you seen Thad yet this morning, Double Trouble?" he called out.

"You promised that you wouldn't call me things like that anymore," I grumbled at his back.

He turned around. "I forgot," he said to Paige, not me. "Everybody calls you Double Trouble, you know."

"No, I didn't know," Paige said.

He squinted at her. "Oh, heck, I did it again. It's only you, isn't it?"

It didn't take a genius to see that he'd hurt Paige's feelings, so I tried to change the subject. "Why are you looking for Thad?" I asked.

"I left my homework at his place and he was supposed to bring it to school today. He's usually here by now. Or did your big dog eat him up?"

"He hasn't been to the house since Bear learned to heel," I said, trying to act as if I didn't care. Once Thad had seen that Bear was learning everything she was supposed to know—and Mrs. Brier wasn't going to abuse her—he stopped coming to our house. I had hoped that he'd develop an interest in me, but he didn't. In fact, he seemed to go out of his way to avoid me.

After Colin left, Paige said, "He likes you an awful lot."

I couldn't look straight at her so I busied myself with the books stacked in my locker. "He's crazy about the idea of having two of *you*, that's all."

"No, I don't think so."

I faced her then. "As far as I'm concerned, that's all it is and that's all it's ever going to be. I need a best pal more than I need a boyfriend right now."

She looked so sober that I was afraid she'd end up crying. "I guess we're in the same predicament then. I have a hunch you like Thad, and he's let you down."

I shrugged and slammed my locker door shut. "He didn't exactly let me down. He was only coming by the house to help out with the puppy and to make sure that we weren't doing something awful to her."

"You mean to make sure Mrs. Brier wasn't doing something awful," Paige said. "You know he always trusted you with the dog."

"Maybe," I said. "I kept trying to prove to him that I'd be really good for Bear, but the harder I tried, the more suspicious he seemed."

And speaking of Thad, there he was, coming toward us from the other end of the hall.

"Colin's looking for you," Paige said as he passed us.

"He caught up with me but thanks anyway, Paige."

If he noticed me—and how could he help it?—he didn't let it show.

"He was probably in a hurry," Paige said, apologizing for him.

"Sure," I said unhappily. "If I brought Bear to school, then he'd notice me."

49

"So would Mr. Stark," Paige responded, laughing.

We walked to our first class and settled into our seats. The bell rang and seconds later the school public address system clicked on. As he did every morning, Mr. Stark made several announcements, yelling so loud that he created feedback. The kids in class started shouting, "Quiet! Quiet!" and the teacher finally turned down the volume.

The last announcement was more of a threat. Mr. Stark told us that anyone who misbehaved in the cafeteria would be denied the privilege of buying lunch and would have to bring food from home.

"Do you promise?" somebody shouted, and everybody laughed. Another of Mr. Zoppler's loony thoughts for the day followed, and the PA system clicked off.

Paige and I exchanged a long look.

"Why does Mr. Stark hand me these opportunities?" Paige asked, straight-faced.

That afternoon I ran home, put Bear on her leash, and took her to Paige's house. While Bear played in the yard with the family dogs, Paige and I did something creative with a piece of fake fur left over from the coats her mother had made for her little sisters. We worked for two hours, but at the end, we had a fat white cat with very stiff legs and two felt crosses for eyes. We put the cat on its back and called Mrs. Worth into the sewing room.

"What do you think?" Paige asked her. "Does this look like a somewhat deceased kitty?"

Mrs. Worth laughed, but she shook her head, too. "That's really awful. What do you two have in mind? I almost believed that it was a dead cat until I saw those silly crosses where its eyes ought to be."

"We got the idea about the crosses from cartoons," I explained. "Anybody who gets close will see right away that it's not a real cat."

"But what are you going to do with it, Paige? Use it at your Halloween party?" Mrs. Worth picked up the cat and stroked it absentmindedly.

"It's sort of a Halloween joke," Paige said vaguely. "We'll get a big laugh from the kids with it."

"Maybe," Mrs. Worth said doubtfully as she looked down into the cat's face.

Before she left, Mrs. Worth invited me for dinner, so I called home and left a message with Mrs. Brier for my mother. Mrs. Brier listened, but she slammed down the phone without saying good-bye.

"I wish I knew why she's so mean," I said to Paige.

"I'll bet she didn't want Dr. Carver to marry again," Paige said. "Maybe she's afraid she'll be fired. She's worked there for as long as I can remember."

We were sitting by the kitchen window, watching Bear bouncing around the yard with a stick. "Did you know Tracey's mother?" I asked.

"No, she left so long ago that I can't remember anything about her. Mom said that she was really strange, though. Incredibly vain and selfish. She didn't take very good care of Tracey, either. When she ran off, everybody thought that Dr. Carver and Tracey would be better off. He hired Mrs. Brier to take care of Tracey, and she stayed on even after Tracey didn't need her any more."

I sighed. "Then Tracey ought to act like Mrs. Brier's her grandmother or something, but she doesn't. I guess she likes Mrs. Brier in spite of how crabby she is, but nobody in that house seems to have any real feelings about anything."

Paige looked astonished. "Doesn't Dr. Carver love your mom?"

"Sure. You can tell he does. And he loves Tracey, too. But he's so . . . so formal! And so is Tracey."

"Your mom seems pretty quiet, too."

"Yes," I said, suddenly miserable. "I'm the odd one out, I guess. Too noisy. Too excitable. Too messy."

"You and Bear," Paige said.

Both of us laughed. It was impossible to stay moody in her house.

The next day Paige smuggled the cat into the cafeteria at the beginning of second lunch before most of the kids arrived. She bought a serving of the day's special, spaghetti and meatballs, and put it on the table closest to the entrance, then laid the cat on its back beside the plate.

The result was better than we had imagined. The kids went crazy. The kitchen staff was furious.

Mr. Stark arrived as Colin was conducting a funeral for the cat. "What is going on?" he asked Colin.

"There's been a death in the cafeteria," Colin said soberly. "We suspect that it was murder."

"Murder by meatball," Thad contributed, surprising me.

"Who did it?" Mr. Stark demanded.

"The cook," somebody yelled.

Mr. Stark was outraged. "No, no! I mean who brought this cat in here? Who set this up?"

He saw me trying not to laugh. "You, Paige Worth, get to my office immediately."

"Okay," Paige said, and she marched toward the door.

"No, no!" Mr. Stark cried. He pointed at me. "You. Heather."

"Okay," I said and I started for the door where Paige waited.

"Do you want the corpse?" Colin asked helpfully, holding up the cat by its tail. "And the evidence?" He picked up the plate with his other hand.

"Or an eyewitness?" Thad stepped forward.

Thad, Colin, Paige, and I spent most of the afternoon

in the office. Even though Paige and I tried to explain that Thad and Colin had nothing to do with the cat, all four of us ended up in the same predicament. Mr. Stark phoned our parents, ranted at them for a while, and then decreed that we would not be allowed to buy lunch in the cafeteria for the rest of the semester.

I don't think it occurred to him that the real punishment would have been for him to order us to buy lunch every day and then eat it. I should have felt guilty about teasing him, but it was such a relief to laugh. At home there was nothing going on but sober silence, yards and yards of it.

To celebrate, the four of us went to Paige's house for ice cream after school, after stopping by my place to pick up Bear.

"I didn't mean to get you in trouble," I told Thad.

He shrugged. "The school needs a little excitement now and then."

"I can't wait to write my cousin about this," I said, spooning up the last of my ice cream.

"You write to her about everything, don't you?" he asked.

"Sure."

"I suppose she thinks that Fox Crossing usually is a dull place," he said.

"Of course not," I said, but I wasn't sure exactly what Amelia did think. My letters were full of complaints about Fox Crossing now. Her letters in response only encouraged me to hang in there and be patient. She didn't commit herself to an opinion about anything but the principal's thoughts for the day. She thought those were hilarious.

"But you still want to go back to Seattle," Thad said. He didn't look at me. He looked down at Bear, who was sleeping at his feet.

Back to Seattle, to Amelia's house, to love and fun and caring? "I suppose so," I said.

He shrugged and walked across the room to where Paige and Colin were helping her little sisters with a jigsaw puzzle. There was no point in trying to explain, so I didn't say anything more. He wouldn't have understood anyway. It wasn't only that I was bored in my new home. I wanted to go back to Seattle because my new home didn't come even close to the new life I'd wanted.

When I left Paige's house, I went home to a brief discussion with Will and Mom about the incident at school, and then to a long evening of clocks ticking and Mrs. Brier slamming pans around in the kitchen.

It sounds stupid, but I would have felt loved if someone—anyone—had yelled at me about what I did in the cafeteria. Amelia would have lost her allowance and been grounded for two weeks.

I was living in the dead zone.

Chapter 6

October was a beautiful month in Fox Crossing, but the weather was much colder, and by Halloween there was snow on the ground.

Paige was giving a big Halloween party, so Bear and I spent every afternoon and nearly all of each weekend at her house, while I helped her make plans. I was there so much that her mother automatically set a place for me at the dinner table and filled a pan with dog food for Bear. Sometimes I forgot to call home to tell anyone that I was having dinner with Paige.

Well, what did it matter? Bear and I didn't fit in at the Carver house and I was certain that everyone would be relieved if we didn't come home any more often than was absolutely necessary. We made too much noise, spilled things, and tracked in dirt. And there seemed to be no end to the amount of confusion we could cause. No, that's not exactly right. Bear didn't cause the confusion—I did.

Here's a perfect example. A week before Halloween, Colin's father offered half of his pumpkin crop to us for party jack-o'-lanterns. In Colin's hearing, I volunteered to carve them, but afterward I changed my mind when Paige told me what a great job her dad could do. A few days later Colin, in a hurry, passed me in the hall and called out, "Where should I deliver the pumpkins, Double Trouble? Your house or hers?" I was in a hurry, too, so I answered, "Hers!" and thought he knew that he was talking to me, Heather, and would deliver the pumpkins to Paige.

The pumpkins ended up on my front porch, and the world practically came to an end.

I'd been at Paige's until late that afternoon, Tracey had gone to the library, and Mom and Will were attending a faculty dinner at the college, so only Mrs. Brier was home. She, rude as usual, decided not to answer the doorbell, so Colin simply unloaded a mountain of muddy pumpkins on the front porch and left.

When I got home, Mrs. Brier was having a fit in the kitchen, Will was calling all over town trying to find out where the pumpkins had come from, and Mom was carrying them around to the back porch with Tracey's help.

Paige, who'd walked home with me, laughed. "I'll bet you all thought that the trick-or-treating had already started," she told Will after we'd explained.

He smiled his quiet smile. "I must confess that I'd forgotten about Halloween," he said.

Mom wasn't smiling. "Oh, Heather," she said simply.

"But nobody was hurt!" I exclaimed, stung by her expression. "It was just a little mistake, not a catastrophe. If Mrs. Brier didn't always make such a huge, silly fuss about everything, there wouldn't have been any problem at all!"

We knew Mrs. Brier had heard me, because a pan hit the sink with such a bang that it must have chipped the enamel.

Mom raised her eyebrows and rolled her eyes.

"You know, Heather's right," Tracey said. She was smiling faintly. "We know where the pumpkins came from and there's no sense in Mrs. Brier's banging things around like that."

Her father shrugged. "She hates surprises."

"Heather won't provide any more of them," Mom said.

"But Heather didn't even know that Colin was going to leave the pumpkins here!" Paige protested.

"She's right, Marsha," Tracey told Mom placidly.

I really appreciated her support, although I couldn't help wishing she were a little more emphatic about it. But then, Tracey was never very emphatic about anything, and this was as rebellious as she ever got. It had an effect, however.

Will strolled out to the kitchen to speak to Mrs. Brier and the banging and clattering stopped. Things might have settled down then if Colin hadn't chosen that moment to come back to check on the pumpkins, saw that they were all gone, and concluded that they'd been stolen.

He hammered on the door, shouting, "Hey, Heather, they're gone! Somebody took 'em! Heather!"

I let him in and explained the situation as well as I could. Nobody ever accused Colin of being the silent type. The whole mess struck him as hilarious.

"I'll bet you thought you were going to have a life-time supply of pumpkin pies," he told us.

"No, we were afraid that the party plans had been changed and it was going to be held here," Tracey said.

I could see that the moment it was out of her mouth she realized what she'd said, and her face turned red.

"Oh, I'm sorry," she said. "I didn't mean it the way it sounded."

I believed her—at least I tried to—but that didn't help. I was so upset and embarrassed that I was afraid I'd cry

57

right in front of everybody. And unfortunately my embarrassment turned into a kind of defensive anger before I could stop it.

"No, I wouldn't do anything so stupid as trying to give a party in good old Dismal Gulch," I said. I grabbed Bear's collar and started for the stairs.

"Heather!" Mom said sharply.

But I wouldn't turn back. "Good night, Paige," I called down to her. "I'm sorry about this. Good night, Colin. Please take the pumpkins over to Paige's house where everybody has a sense of humor."

And I slammed my bedroom door shut.

Mother came right up to talk to me but I refused to discuss it. All I'd say was that I was tired of explaining and apologizing for living, and I asked her to go away and leave me alone. I only went downstairs twice all evening—to let Bear out into the backyard for a few minutes each time.

"I've never been more unhappy," I wrote Amelia. "The Carvers and my mother think I do everything wrong. Maybe I do. But all I wanted was a normal, ordinary family, not a house full of department store mannequins. Sometimes I wonder why I never noticed before that my own mother never says more than ten words at a time. It's true! When I look back, I can't remember ever having a very long conversation with her—certainly not like I had with Aunt Ellen.

"It can't be *all* my fault, can it? Tell me the truth, Amelia. Am I doing something wrong here?"

I signed the letter, "Miserable in Fox Crossing."

On the morning of the party, Paige went off to her hairdresser's to get beautiful, and I, who was too depressed to care how I looked, took Bear for a long walk around our part of town. Most of the snow had melted and the rest had frozen, so the streets glittered like silver. My pup and I finally gave up walking where it was slippery and tramped into the park. I threw a stick for her and she brought it back sometimes and lay down to chew on it the rest of the time.

I sat on a bench, huddling inside my jacket and brooding about everything. If there had been a way that I could have packed up and moved back to Seattle that morning, I would have done it.

Somebody called out, "Hi!" and I turned on the bench and saw Thad Shipton being pulled across the frozen grass by Bear's sister, who'd been named Heidi. Bear rushed off to her and the two of them ran in crazy circles for a while.

Thad sat down next to me. "I'm glad Bear didn't forget her sister."

The dogs were so happy to see each other that I had tears in my eyes. "I guess I should have tried to get them together before this," I said.

Thad nodded soberly.

"Bear's getting along very well," I said quickly, before he could ask. "Mrs. Brier hasn't done anything mean to her."

"Yeah," Thad said. I didn't think that he was agreeing with me. He was only acknowledging that I'd said something. "Well," he added slowly as he watched Bear, "she looks like she's in good shape. You're not giving her real bones, are you?"

"Never," I said. "Only nylon ones, and a special big one that Will found in a pet store. It's sort of like rubber, only she can't chew off pieces."

"Good," Thad said. "Real bones are bad."

"I know."

We sat in stupid silence for a long, long time. Bear and Heidi played until they were exhausted, and then they wandered back toward us. Both Thad and I bent at the same time to put the leashes back on our dogs.

"Are you coming to Paige's party tonight?" I asked him, more to fill in the silence than out of real curiosity. I'd pretty much given up any hope of ever attracting any attention from him that wasn't centered on whether or not I was taking good care of Bear. I saw him nearly every day, usually sat at his table in the cafeteria, and we were part of the same group that went to movies together or out for hamburgers. But we stayed practically strangers.

"I'll show up at the party for a while, anyway," he said as he got to his feet. He looked around vaguely, as if he wasn't certain where he ought to direct his gaze since he certainly didn't want to look straight at me.

"Fine," I said. "I guess I'll see you later, then."

He nodded, but he didn't smile, and as he led Heidi away I wished that I'd been able to think of something to say that would have made me sound interesting to him.

But Bear distracted me then. When she realized that her sister was leaving, she went wild, lunging at the end of her leash and bellowing. She was too big for me to pick up, so the only thing I could do was sit down beside her and wrap both my arms around her until Thad and Heidi disappeared and she calmed down.

We were both subdued when we got home.

Mrs. Brier often took Saturdays off, as well as Sundays, and so she was gone that day. Mom was spending the entire day at the free clinic, Tracey had gone someplace with her John, and so Will and I had lunch alone at the kitchen table. I was still a little embarrassed about how I'd behaved the other night, so I made up my mind to try to smooth things over with my stepfather.

He'd fixed hot dogs and chili—which happened to be one of my favorite cold-weather lunches.

"Your mother wouldn't think much of this meal," he said, smiling faintly as he set my food in front of me.

"I know. She doesn't count chili sauce as a vegetable. Or pickle relish, either." I grinned at him and then took a huge, satisfying bite of my hot dog.

"Here's a cup of hot chocolate. Maybe the cocoa counts as a vegetable," Will said soberly as he put my cup down on the table.

"If not, then the marshmallows will."

I was doing my best to keep from laughing out loud, waiting for him to laugh first. But he didn't. When I dared take a quick look at him, he was chewing thoughtfully and looking out the kitchen window.

Uncle Jock would have watched me watching him, and both of us would have waited for the other one to crack up first. But both of us would have begun laughing at the same time. We always did.

Inwardly I sighed a big sigh. Will was nothing like Uncle Jock. I was waiting for something that was never going to happen.

The afternoon mail brought me a long letter from Amelia. "You're breaking my heart," she wrote. "If you were happy, maybe I could stand your being so far away, but you're miserable and so am I."

Tracey came home later, excited because she and John had found an old arrowhead in a box of junk at a flea market. She'd forgotten to pick up her dry cleaning, though, so she couldn't wear her favorite dress that night. I told her to wear one of mine, if she saw something in my closet that she liked, but she refused.

"It'll serve me right for forgetting the dry cleaning," she said. "I seem to get more absentminded every day. Anyway, I'm too big for your clothes. But thanks for offering."

I would have been pleased if I could have convinced myself that she wouldn't forget about me, too, as soon as I was out of sight.

Chapter 7

Thought for the day: We learn more from bad times than we do from good. (Pause.) I wish I knew why.
Harold Z. Zoppler, Principal
Fox Crossing High School

Paige's party wouldn't start until eight, but I was ready to leave home by six because I'd promised to help in any way I could. Tracey and John, who were going out to dinner with friends and then on to a double-feature horror show, offered to give me a ride to the Worths' house, and I accepted gratefully.

Tracey came out of her bedroom just as I was starting down the stairs. "Are you going as a black cat?" she asked me.

I was wearing Mom's old black turtleneck sweater and my black jeans. "No. Everybody goes to Paige's Halloween parties dressed in black, she says. After we get there, she'll hand out paper bags with masks and hats or wigs for us. She doesn't even know what each of us will be because her sisters are the ones who fill the bags. Doesn't that sound like fun?"

"Sounds different," Tracey said. "They must buy out half the stores in town."

"No, Mrs. Worth told me that the whole family collects masks and different kinds of head coverings all year long."

Bear saw me zipping up my jacket and yelped in panic. She hated being left behind. Will grabbed her up—he was the only one in the family who could still lift her easily—and took her out to the kitchen. "Let's split a pizza," he told her. I heard Mom tell him that pizza wasn't good for either one of them.

"Things are so much nicer when Mrs. Brier isn't around," I blurted without thinking.

Tracey shrugged. "She'll learn to accept you in time."

I wanted to say that maybe Mrs. Brier ought to be worrying about how long it would take for Mom and me to accept her. But I kept that sassy idea to myself. It was apparent to me by then that Mrs. Brier was a permanent fixture in the household.

John drove up then, and we climbed in his car. When they let me off at the Worths' house, they asked me if I'd need a ride home.

"I don't know yet," I told them. I'd had a demented and brief hope that Thad would ask to take me home after the party, but since I couldn't count on that, I added, "I'll call Mom if I can't get a ride from anyone else."

That satisfied Tracey, so they drove off, and I ran up the porch steps. Paige yanked open the door before I could even knock.

"Everything has gone wrong and I wish I was dead," she grumbled, pulling me inside. "This is going to be the worst party the world has ever seen."

Her mother, laughing, took my jacket and hung it up. "Paige says that every year. Nothing's gone wrong—at least, not yet—and it won't be the worst party in the world, either."

I saw several boxes next to the door, each one filled with paper bags. "Are those the masks?"

"And wigs, hats, scarves, eye patches, makeup—oh, just about anything you can name," Mrs. Worth told me. "We only hand out half masks, because otherwise those youngsters couldn't eat without the others finding out who they were."

"All the kids do for the first few minutes is work on finding out who everybody else is," Paige told me. "Some of them are really clever about fooling the rest of us."

"Where are your sisters? Won't they be at the party, too?" I asked. The house was quieter than it usually was. Paige's little sisters were as noisy as my cousins. Even the dogs seemed to be missing.

"Sisters and dogs went to the Alexanders' down the block," Paige said. "There's going to be a kid and dog party there."

"I hope Bear doesn't hear about it. She hated being left home tonight."

But Paige wasn't listening to me. She suddenly did a little dance in the hall and yanked on her hair. "I'm really going crazy this time, Heather. I want everything to be perfect, but it's going to be awful, I just know it."

I laughed along with Mrs. Worth. "You've got nearly two hours to go before people start coming," I reminded her. "There's plenty of time for everything."

I followed them through the house. Mr. Worth had carved the pumpkins into jack-o'-lanterns, really clever ones, and they sat about the big living room and dining room with candles inside, all ready to be lit. "The pumpkins are wonderful," I said.

"Isn't Dad good?" Paige asked.

I looked around at the funny faces as I nodded, and I tried to imagine Will spending all the hours it must have taken to do the work. What a silly idea. He might have agreed to try, but he'd have either forgotten about it or begged off.

Micky and Sandy came a few minutes later to help, too. The four of us and Mrs. Worth worked in the kitchen, preparing enough food to feed the crowd.

Sandy carried bowl after bowl of salad into the dining room as the time grew nearer for the first guests to arrive. Mr. Worth brought home several bags of ice and emptied them into buckets. Micky, balancing two trays of glasses, passed me with my load of soft drink bottles. I counted six chocolate cakes with orange or yellow frosting on the dining room sideboard.

"It's nearly eight!" Paige cried suddenly, scaring me silly. "Quick, get out your disguises."

We ran for the bags. "Are we supposed to hide from each other now?" I asked.

"Oh, that rule's not for the kitchen help," Sandy said. "Everybody else will duck down the basement steps or into closets or go back out on the porch while they get fixed up." She pulled from the bag a bushy black wig and thick glasses, several tubes of makeup, a bandage, and a stick-on plastic scar. "Oh, no," she exclaimed. "I'm going to look like someone who was trampled by a herd of cattle."

"And I'll look like the one who let them get away," I said as I displayed a cowboy hat, an ugly mask complete with a shaggy moustache, and a bandanna.

Paige's bag contained a black veil, a ridiculous red satin hat with a bunch of cherries glued to one side, and a gaudy glass necklace. "Who am I?" She dropped the veil over her head and plopped the hat on top.

"I don't know," Micky said, "but I think we're blood relatives." She showed a large, feather headdress, a long, blond wig, and a purple satin mask with sequins.

"What if a boy had ended up with that bag?" I asked.

"Too bad," Paige answered, laughing as she fastened the hideous necklace and adjusted it to hang over the tails of the black veil. "You wear what you get, no matter how silly it looks. That's part of the fun. Last year Colin ended up with an ugly white wig and a mask with a big red nose."

"But you loved him anyway," Micky said complacently as she adjusted her mask. "Do I look beautiful?"

"You look awful and you know it," Sandy told her, laughing. "Hey, I hear a car!"

"Showtime," Paige muttered. "Is everything going to be all right? Tell me, quick!" She was so panicky that I felt sorry for her.

"It's perfect!" Micky said.

"Perfect," Sandy echoed.

The doorbell rang and my first Fox Crossing party began. For the next few hours, I wouldn't give Mrs. Brier and the Carver house another thought because I was in the middle of a crowd and that was what I liked best.

I was so busy helping Paige that I didn't take much time to look around for a while. But one of the first things I looked for when I could was a tall boy, maybe the tallest one there, who had to be Thad. When I finally found him, I had trouble recognizing him, though, because he was wearing a floppy black hat over a scraggly gray wig, a big plastic nose and an eye patch. And an enormous earring.

"Hi, there, Captain Kidd," I said as I passed him a platter of sandwiches.

He glanced at me only briefly. "Thanks for the grub, cowboy."

I wanted to tell him who I was, but that would spoil the fun, so I carried off the platter to the next boy, who was wearing a scarf with frizzy blond bangs hanging out the front and a frog mask. "Would you like another sandwich, Miss Frog," I asked, trying to disguise my voice.

"Mr. Frog to you, pal." I recognized Colin's gruff voice. "You sound like you've got a cold. The cowboy's hoarse!" He started laughing and I couldn't help joining in.

"Paige?" he asked quickly. "Is that you? Sure it is. I recognize the laugh."

"Horse laugh," I said in my disguised voice, and I hurried away before he could be sure of who I was.

The family room was packed with dancers, but a steady stream of kids marched through the dining room, filling paper plates with food. Paige cut cakes and Sandy added a scoop of ice cream to each serving. Micky and Mr. Worth carried in more soft drinks. I opened two extra cans of olives to refill the big bowl in the center of the table.

Someone nudged my shoulder. "Yes?" I said in response, without looking up.

"You've been so busy with the food that you haven't had a chance to dance." It was Colin. "How about it?"

"I can't right now," I said. Oh, dear, I thought. I hope Paige isn't seeing this. She's probably guessed that this is Colin. And he thinks he's trying to rescue her from kitchen duty.

"I didn't mean just tonight," he said. "I can see that you've got your hands full with the party. But what about the Thanksgiving dance next month?"

I smiled as I gathered up some crumpled napkins. I was sure he thought I was Paige. "We can talk about it," I said, and then I rushed away to the kitchen before I gave myself away.

The room was empty for the first time all evening, but Paige would be back any second. Now how was I going to handle this? Should I tell her that Colin thought she was the cowboy?

Colin came in right behind me. "When can we talk about it, Heather?" he said. "Can I take you home tonight?"

Oh, no. I turned to face him quickly. "Sorry, Colin," I said. "I've already made arrangements for getting home."

"Then about the dance? You said we could talk about it. Does that mean you'll go with me?"

Micky and Sandy came in then, laughing, grabbing for bags of potato chips. I left the room with them, without answering Colin. I had no idea of what I was going to do and I needed a chance to think.

By eleven, the family room was even more crowded. I had time to dance then, and danced with lots of boys, but Thad didn't ask me and I was too nervous to ask him.

Colin insisted on knowing how I was getting home, so I told him my mother was coming for me. Making any other arrangement would have been too complicated, since Colin was watching me most of the time. When he finally wandered off to dance with Sandy for a while, I knew I'd better get it over with and call Mom. There was no chance downstairs for privacy, so I asked Mrs. Worth if I could use the upstairs phone.

Just because life can be completely impossible sometimes, Thad was waiting for me to return downstairs, and the first thing he said was, "Can I take you home?"

I wanted to shout, "What took you so long!" Instead, I explained that my mother was coming for me.

He was still wearing the eye patch, but not the ugly nose, and he looked marvelous, so tall and lean and sort of shaggy. Definitely huggable. I was getting spots in front of my eyes.

"Your mother is driving you home?" he asked. "You could have asked someone here for a ride. Lots of the kids drove themselves."

"I was hoping somebody would think of asking me sooner," I said, and I couldn't help sounding grouchy. Obviously my brain had clicked off, leaving my mouth in charge of my future.

He looked uncomfortable. "You were always so busy. And Colin hangs around all the time."

It was true. Oh, darn, darn, darn!

"Bad planning, I guess," I said.

"You could call your mother and tell her not to come," Thad suggested awkwardly.

And Colin would see me leave with Thad. Things had become too complicated.

"I'd better not do that," I said. I glanced at my watch. "Mom might be getting ready to leave now."

Thad nodded. "Yes. Well, sorry. Maybe we could dance until she gets here."

I liked that idea, but we didn't have much time together before I saw Sandy and Micky gathering up paper plates and leftovers and carrying them to the kitchen. "I've got to help them," I told Thad regretfully.

"You're a good dancer, Heather," he said.

I didn't believe him but it was certainly nice to hear. "Thanks. Maybe we can do it again sometime."

But all he said was, "Sure," and then I was embarrassed because he probably thought that I was hinting around.

Well, I was. Admitting it to myself embarrassed me even more.

Mom didn't arrive until a little after twelve, and by that time, as a signal that the party was over, Mrs. Worth was bustling around blowing out the candles that were still burning in some the jack-o'-lanterns. Anyone who wanted to take home one of Mr. Worth's works of art was welcome to do so. There was one by the front door that I especially liked, but when I went to get it, I found Mom there, holding it and laughing.

"Do you mind if I take this?" Mom asked Paige's dad.

"Strange you should pick that one," Mr. Worth said. "I had Will in mind while I was working on it."

Mom laughed and I could tell that she was sincerely

69

amused, but her laugh was quiet. A true Carver laugh, I thought.

But, I realized suddenly, Mom always laughed like that. Gently and softly.

I was the one who howled and got tears in my eyes. Like Amelia, her sisters, and Uncle Jock. The Whitneys didn't just have grass green eyes. They laughed louder and longer than other people. And at more things.

I was a Whitney. But my mother was a Carver now. So I was all alone in Fox Crossing.

Chapter 8

Thought for the day: Most things you worry about never happen. But some of them do. (Sigh)

Harold Z. Zoppler, Principal
Fox Crossing High School

The next day Paige called me about noon and asked me if I'd had a good time at the party and did I want to come over and help them eat leftovers. Bear was invited, too, of course.

Did I ever want to go! Mom and Will had gone for a long walk, Tracey was typing something in her room, and except for the clickety-click coming from upstairs, the house was so quiet that I could hear Bear snoring in the hall.

"I had a wonderful time last night, and I'll be on your porch instantly," I told Paige before I hung up.

I was halfway there before I remembered that Colin had asked me to go to the Thanksgiving dance with him. I guess I'd deliberately pushed that potential disaster out of my mind so I wouldn't have to think about it. Sooner or later Colin would want an answer, and I'd better come up with something. And I'd better tell Paige what had happened.

No! Was I out of my mind? Paige and I were good friends, but we hadn't known each other long enough yet for me to correctly gauge how she would react to learning that the boy she liked had asked me out instead. And not because he had mistaken me for her, either.

71

I slowed and stopped dead on the sidewalk. Bear looked up at me inquiringly, decided that it was time for another nap, and lay down in the snow.

"It's too cold for that," I told her.

She yawned and rolled over on her side.

"No, no, you have to get up now. We're going to Paige's house."

Bear's eyes were closed.

I bent and hoisted her to her feet. She yawned, making a little squeaking noise, and looked up at me as if to say, Can't you make up your mind?

I groaned and trudged on toward Paige's house. What was I going to do? Tell and risk our friendship? Keep quiet and risk her finding out?

She might not find out if I could get Colin aside someplace soon enough and tell him that I couldn't go to the dance with him. Or perhaps I could phone him. Whatever I decided, I'd better do it soon, before he had a chance to tell anyone that he'd asked me or maybe even hint around that I'd agreed to go.

That was the smartest thing to do, I decided.

Too bad I didn't ask the puppy what she thought, because she'd have told me that it was the dumbest thing I could do.

Paige and I ate lunch in the family room with her little sisters, played three video games (I lost all of them), and then we tucked up kids and dogs for long naps and went to Paige's room for a chat. I should have gone home.

For the next two hours Paige talked about Colin. He'd danced with her several times the night before, and she took that to mean that he'd finally developed an interest in her.

"Don't you think I'm right?" she asked me. "He wouldn't have danced with me so many times if he hadn't wanted to. That's what Sandy and Micky think.

72

And maybe, if I hadn't been so busy with the food and everything, he might have danced all the time with me. Don't you think so?"

"You're a terrific dancer," I said, desperate to change the subject. "Would you like to be a professional?"

She stared at me. "No, of course not. I want to work here in Fox Crossing at my grandfather's drugstore, just like Dad does now. Did you know that Grandpa's store is next to the hardware store that Colin's dad owns?"

"You mean you want to be a pharmacist?" I asked. I was more than desperate by now to get her mind off Colin.

"Someday, I guess," she said. "That's too far off. But Colin says he wants to be an engineer. He's not interested in his father's business."

No matter how hard I tried to get her off the subject of Colin, she kept dragging the conversation right back to him. "Where do Thad's parents work?" I asked.

"Hmm?" Paige turned her head to study her hair from first the left, then the right. "Oh, Thad's parents teach at the college. Did you talk to Colin last night? Did he happen to mention me?"

This would have been the perfect time to tell her that he'd asked me to go to the Thanksgiving dance, but I didn't. Instead, I said, "We danced for a minute, but he didn't say much of anything."

For the rest of the time I was there, my mind was filled with the racket of my own thoughts. A dozen times I said that I had to be going home, but Paige always begged me to stay a little while longer. Finally, my misery was ended by a phone call from my mother. I had succeeded in trading one awful situation for another.

"We've been worried about you, Heather," Mom began.

"Sorry," I said hastily. "I'm on my way home now."

73

"Oh, aren't you staying for dinner?" Paige called behind me.

"We'd appreciate your presence at our table," Mom said crossly. "And a little more warning when you do plan to have dinner somewhere else. Mrs. Brier says that even when you do call, it's never until the last minute."

It was true, but I was tense and nervous, so I didn't use my head and shut up while I still had a chance. "Maybe I'd call Mrs. Brier sooner if she wasn't so nasty," I said.

There was one of those awful silences that kids hear from their mothers just before an explosion takes place.

Finally she said, "We'll discuss this when we don't have to do it over the telephone. Do you need a ride? It's almost dark."

I looked out the window and saw that she was right, but I declined her offer. "Bear and I will run and be there right away."

She said good-bye and hung up.

"Are you in trouble?" Paige asked as she brought my jacket.

"I think so." I fastened Bear's leash to her collar and started for the door.

"I guess she doesn't like your staying here so much," Paige said. "I sorta got that impression last night."

I whirled around. "What do you mean? Did she say something last night?" It wasn't like Mom to say nasty things to people.

Paige shrugged. "Mom offered her some cake to take home, and your mom said that we fed you so much she was embarrassed about it. That's all. She was laughing when she said it."

My face burned. "She's right. I eat here all the time. Your parents must be sick of me."

"No! They love having company. Both Mom and Dad

have said a dozen times that you're just like another daughter to them."

Suddenly and stupidly I began crying.

"What's wrong?" Paige asked. "Did I hurt your feelings?"

I shook my head and dug a tissue out of my pocket. "I like being here more than I like being home, but I've been making a pest out of myself."

"What's wrong at home?" Paige asked.

I shook my head again. "I'm not sure you'll understand. I know I should be happy there, but I'd expected something different. A home like you've got. Like my cousin has."

Paige looked bewildered. "Dr. Carver's always seemed so kind. And Tracey may be a little dull, but she's like her dad. At least I thought so until now."

"It's not them, it's me! They're both nice to me, and the house is beautiful. It's just not what I'd always dreamed I'd have. It's too quiet, and they're not as casual as my aunt and uncle are. And your parents, too. I mean they don't laugh very much. Or maybe it's that they don't laugh at the same things." I stopped and blew my nose. "You must think I'm an idiot."

But Paige shook her head slowly. "No, and I know what you mean about the Carver house being quiet and formal. They're just different, that's all."

"My mother fits in but I don't," I said. "I make too much noise going up and down the stairs, and the doors I close always seem to slam even when I don't mean for them to. And I spill things—this morning I spilled a whole bottle of shampoo on the bathroom floor, and I used towels to mop up the mess, and then when I put the towels in the washer, the washer overflowed with suds, all over the laundry room floor. If Mrs. Brier had seen it, she would have killed me. And Will just—he just *pitied* me."

Paige threw her arms around me and hugged me until I could scarcely breathe. "You've only been here a couple of months," she said. "Things will get better. You wait and see. And nobody pities you. What a crazy idea."

I felt better by the time I left, but as soon as I walked in the Carver house I was ready to cry all over again.

Mom, Will, Tracey, and John were waiting for me. Dinner was on the table—and it was already getting cold. I couldn't even take time out for crying without spoiling everything for everybody else!

At Amelia's house, this would have turned into a big discussion at the table, with lots of arguing and laughing and maybe even some tears, but by dessert everybody would be back to loving everybody else again.

At my house we ate in almost complete silence. Once John said that he certainly did like barbecued chicken and Will said, "Thanks, John. It's the only thing I can cook, except for hot dogs and chili. Thank heaven we have Mrs. Brier here most of the week."

"Mom's a good cook," I said.

Everybody stared at me. "But your mother works every afternoon at the clinic and we couldn't expect her to fix dinner, too," Will said.

Why didn't Mom say that she'd always worked and then come home and fixed dinner—with a little help from me? No, she just kept right on cutting up a piece of chicken and chewing each bite a thousand times. She never looked at me once.

We finished the meal in total silence then. It was obvious that I was the only one upset by this. Everybody else was probably thinking great big important thoughts about life on other planets or ways to reduce the national debt.

We had dessert in Will's den, just as we always did, and afterward everybody else played word games. I said

I had a headache and went upstairs with Bear. We fell asleep on my bed.

Mom woke me up later. She sat down in the chair next to my bed and said, "We have to talk."

"About eating dinner at the Worths'?"

"About your attitude in general," she said. "I know that you need time to adjust to living in a different town and having a stepfather—"

"I like Will. And Tracey, too."

She sighed. "I know you do. But living in a family situation is different from living alone in an apartment with only your mother."

"I like families."

Mom had clasped her hands together in her lap, and she looked down at them now. "You like Amelia's family. I've always known how you idealized them. But not everyone wants to live that way."

"What's wrong with it?" I demanded.

She looked up at me then. "Nothing. And there's nothing wrong with the way Will and Tracey live, either."

"Silent dinners and dessert in the den with word games," I said. "Nobody talks and nobody laughs. Nobody even watches TV in this house. You can hear the clocks ticking in the afternoon. And Mrs. Brier is awful!"

Mom's face flushed. "She's difficult, I grant you that. But she's been here for years. She practically raised Tracey. . . ."

"Tracey's seventeen! She doesn't need a baby-sitter."

"Mrs. Brier's here and she'll stay. You might as well accept that, because I have."

I leaned toward her. "You don't like her either, do you?"

Mom sighed. "I knew she'd be a part of my life when

I agreed to marry Will. We'll learn to accept each other.''

I threw myself flat on the bed. "Why? Give me one reason why she has to be here.''

Mom didn't answer for a long time. Then she said, "I don't know myself. Will won't talk about the time when Tracey's mother left them. He said only that if it hadn't been for Mrs. Brier, he doesn't know what he would have done.''

"Let her get her own husband and child," I said angrily.

"She has a husband. That's why she goes home every night. She's not here because of Will. It's because of Tracey.''

"That doesn't make sense," I argued. "I'm not even sure that Tracey likes her. Sometimes she's really hard on Mrs. Brier.''

Mom blinked soberly. "Tracey isn't sentimental. I suppose her early experiences account for that.''

I still didn't understand anything. "What early experiences?" I asked.

"Her mother was neglectful. That's all I know, Heather. So I think you should try to be a little understanding of the circumstances here.''

Suddenly I felt ashamed of myself. I grabbed Mom and hugged her and apologized. "I'll do better, I promise," I told her.

And I meant it. I even wrote to Amelia that night, telling her that I was going to try harder than ever.

But the next afternoon something happened that was so awful that things went straight from Bad to Unbearable. And I learned to *really* hate Mrs. Brier.

Chapter 9

Thought for the day: Some of you think that the
teachers are here only because it's a warm place to
wait for payday. Well, let me tell you that there's a
lot less going on here than meets the eye, and we
should be grateful for that.

Harold Z. Zoppler, Principal
Fox Crossing High School

Before school the next morning I tried to solve the
problem of Colin's invitation to the dance. I phoned him
and said I couldn't go, and I asked him not to tell anyone
he'd asked me.

"Are you going with someone else, Heather?"

"No, that's not it," I said, trying to keep my voice
down so no one in the house would hear. "I just can't
go with you. Please, please don't mention to anyone that
you asked me."

"What difference does it make?" he complained. "I
don't understand any of this. Are you going or aren't
you? Are you waiting for someone else to ask you?"

I'd been hoping that Thad would ask me even though
I knew he wouldn't, but I wasn't about to admit it.
"No," I told Colin, "I'm not going to the dance. That's
not the important thing. You've got to promise that you
won't tell anyone that you asked me to go."

"Well, I'm sure not going to advertise that I asked
you and you turned me down," he said, trying hard to
laugh. "But I still don't understand. If you're not going

with anybody else—or waiting for some other guy to ask you—why can't you go with me?''

I couldn't believe he was so dense that he didn't suspect that Paige liked him.

''Look,'' I said, gathering up all the patience I had left, ''don't you think some other girl might be hurt when she finds out that you asked me first?''

''What other girl?'' he demanded. ''I'm not going to ask anybody else. What are you talking about?''

I sighed. ''You ought to ask somebody else, and you shouldn't tell her that you asked me first. Understand?''

''No,'' he said bluntly. ''You aren't making any sense. I can't even think of any other girl right now.''

''But who did you like before I moved here?''

I had to wait for him to think that over. ''Well, I don't know. I liked a lot of girls. . . .''

''Then you must still like them, so pick one of them to take to the dance,'' I said, and I hung up before I lost my temper.

Good grief. Colin had never struck me as being particularly stupid, but why couldn't he see that the logical thing for him to do now was to ask Paige?

To make things worse, it was probably the first time any of the girls in my particular group of friends had been asked out on a real date. I should have been excited and eager to tell everybody that maybe now, at long last, the sophomore girls were going to begin actually dating instead of just going along with a gang of kids to a movie or mixer. After all, if Colin began asking girls out, then wouldn't the rest of the boys follow? Instead of Colin's invitation being a hopeful sign, though, it was shaping up to be bad news all the way around.

I was halfway to school with Tracey before I remembered that Colin hadn't promised that he wouldn't tell anyone that he'd invited me first. All he'd said was that he didn't want to advertise my turning him down. Well, that would have to do. I was probably worrying about nothing. I had a tendency to do that.

When I got to school, I found Paige at the center of a crowd of sophomores who were telling her what a great time they'd had at her party. Colin came in while we were still standing there. He gave me a strange look, smiled awkwardly, and wandered off. I couldn't tell if Paige had seen him or not.

The first bell rang and the kids went off in all directions. Sandy and Paige waited while I dumped stuff in my locker, slammed the door shut, and then remembered that I needed two books.

"I can't believe how stupid I am," I said as I dug through my junk.

"Maybe being stupid runs in the family," someone said, with a nasty snicker.

We all turned and saw Darren Pauley and Kix Michaels standing behind us.

How dare they intrude on us? They didn't even know me—they were Tracey's enemies—and they had no right to say anything nasty, anyway. I certainly hadn't been talking to them.

"Darren, don't you just wish that being stupid ran in Heather's family," Sandy said. "My sister told me how much you wanted the scholarship that Tracey won."

Darren's face turned purple and he walked off, jerking like a puppet with tangled strings.

"If you knew what I know, you wouldn't stand there laughing," Kix said to me, and then she waddled after Darren.

"What is she talking about?" I asked Paige and Sandy.

"Don't pay any attention to her," Paige said crisply. "Kix is so nasty she can't stand herself. I can't imagine why Darren's been hanging around with her."

"He doesn't exactly have much choice," Sandy said.

"She's the only senior who likes him. My sister says he's always trying to date the cheerleaders, but nobody will go out with him. Can you believe that he actually asks people what grades they get on their tests? I mean, he compares! Come on, let's go to class."

As we ran down the hall, I asked, "Is he smart? Like Tracey?"

"Almost," Sandy said.

I would have forgotten the whole incident if it hadn't been for what Kix said. If I knew what she knew? What did she mean?

That morning during history, we were assigned big research projects, and Sandy told me she had the perfect reference book for mine. I said I'd drop by her house on my way home to pick it up, but that meant I had to find Tracey fast to be certain that she was going straight home after school to watch Bear. Luckily, I caught up with her outside her physics class, just seconds before the bell rang, and she promised to hurry home to Bear. I still worried about the pup during the two hours each afternoon that Mrs. Brier was supposed to watch her, and I certainly wasn't going to give the old witch any reason to be angry with me, because I was afraid she'd take it out on Bear.

That afternoon, right after lunch, a storm broke over Fox Crossing. The power went out, and there wasn't enough light to read by in class, so we stood at the windows and watched rain blow in heavy sheets. Across the street, a tree fell, hitting a parked car. Another fell a few minutes later, narrowly missing a house. By the time the school day was over, the lights were back on, but no one was in a mood for anything but running home as fast as possible.

I had to stop by Sandy's, so I was prepared to be soaked by the time I reached my house. But I was more than soaked. You could have wrung water out of my clothes.

I hurried through the house toward the laundry room where I was going to hang up my drenched coat. "Hi, Tracey!" I called out.

Tracey didn't answer me, but Bear let out a pitiful cry from the backyard. I yanked open the laundry room door, astonished. Bear was standing outside in the rain, shivering and crying, and when she saw me, she leaped toward me.

Her fur was wet clear to her skin. Without bothering to take off my coat, I grabbed up a pile of clean towels and started rubbing Bear dry. I used every towel, but she was still damp and shivering. I opened the cupboard where Mrs. Brier stored extra blankets and grabbed three. I used one to finish drying Bear, another to wrap her up, and the last one to wrap up myself.

"I'll never forgive them for this," I told the puppy. "Never, never."

It was all I could do to lift Bear, for she was growing to be a huge dog, but I managed. I hauled her up the stairs and put her on my bed, and then I went down the hall to Tracey's room and banged on the door. No answer. I opened the door.

Her books weren't there. Tracey wasn't even home yet! She had forgotten that she was supposed to watch Bear, and Mrs. Brier had obviously gone somewhere and left Bear outside to spite me.

Well, they were going to be sorry!

Bear fell asleep on my bed, so I took a hot shower and put on my warmest clothes. If Bear got sick from being shut out in the storm, I was going to take her to Seattle with me. I was finished with the Carver house and everybody in it.

A few minutes later I heard the front door open and

close. I ran out of my room and leaned over the banister. "Who is it?" I yelled.

"Tracey," Tracey called back.

"You forgot Bear!" I yelled. "How could you have done that? Mrs. Brier went off and left her outside in the storm!"

Tracey walked into the hall below me and looked up. Her face was white. "Bear was out in the rain?"

"Yes!" I yelled. "And it's your fault! You know Mrs. Brier is crazy!"

The front door opened again, and Mrs. Brier came in. She passed by Tracey in the hall and said, "Let me take your coat, Tracey. You're soaked."

"You left Bear outside," I yelled. "Where were you?"

Mrs. Brier smirked at me. "I had to go to the store. You're supposed to be home by three. When you didn't show up, I left."

"Didn't you know the dog was outside?" Tracey asked.

Mrs. Brier shrugged. "Dogs are supposed to be out-side." She carried Tracey's coat off.

Tracey turned wearily toward the stairs. "Is Bear all right, Heather?" she asked.

"Of course not!" I shouted. "She was outside for a long time in that awful storm. How could she be all right?"

"I'm sorry, Heather. I really am." Tracey followed me to my room and looked in at Bear. "Maybe we'd better call the vet." Her words said one thing but the expression on her face said something else. She wasn't really thinking about Bear at all.

"What's wrong with you?" I asked, staring at her. "You're acting weird. I don't think you care about the dog at all."

"Of course I care," she said, blinking behind her

glasses. She patted Bear, who groaned in her sleep. Then, without another word, she left my room and went to her own, shutting the door behind her quietly.

I slammed my door as hard as I could, causing Bear to flinch in her sleep.

This was unreal. And unforgivable. This house was no place for Bear and me to live, not anymore. Nobody cared enough about anybody else. Nobody *felt* anything!

Mom and Will came home early and together, which surprised me, but I took full advantage. I ran downstairs as soon as I heard them come in, to tell them that Mrs. Brier had left poor Bear out in the storm.

Tracey came down when she heard me. "It was partly my fault, Dad," she said. "I should have come straight home from school instead of running to John's to use the phone, but the school phone was out because of the storm and I had to talk to you."

Will held up his hand. "Mrs. Brier knows better than to leave the pup outside. But Bear's probably all right now, so we can put that matter aside for a moment—"

I didn't wait to hear what else he was going to say. "Put it aside!" I cried. "How can you? We still don't know if Bear is going to get sick from being so cold. And Mrs. Brier will do it all over again the next chance she gets. How can you put it aside? Don't you care about anything? Ever?"

"Heather!" Mom said sharply. "Something else has been going on, and it's very serious."

"What could be more serious than deliberately trying to hurt a puppy?" I argued hotly.

Mom and Will exchanged a quick glance, then both of them looked at Tracey.

"She might as well know now," Tracey said. "I'd rather tell her myself than have her learn it at school."

"What are you talking about?" I asked.

Before they had a chance to say anything, Mrs. Brier

came out of the kitchen. "I won't have Heather speaking to me the way she did this afternoon," she said to Will.

Will stared at her for a moment, seeming bewildered. "What happened?"

I couldn't believe it. He'd forgotten about Bear already?

"You people make me sick!" I said furiously. "I wish I'd never come here. I wish I could take Bear and leave here before she's so neglected that something terrible happens to her."

I turned and started up the stairs, crying so hard that I could barely see.

"Heather, come back here," Mom called out to me.

"No!" I shouted. "I don't want to talk to you until I hear you tell Mrs. Brier that what she did was cruel and mean, and that she'd better not ever do anything like that again or she'll be fired!"

I slammed my door again and that time I locked it. Mom came up immediately and tried to come in, but I refused to unlock the door and I refused to listen to her. "I don't care what you have to say," I said loudly enough to be heard downstairs. "And you can tell *them* that I don't care what they have to say, either. Mrs. Brier was wrong, wrong, wrong! I hate her!"

Later, Tracey came up and told me through my door that she was sorry for her part in what had happened to the pup. I didn't answer. When it was time to feed Bear and let her out for a while, I took her downstairs and walked past the den without even looking in at Mom and Will. Will called out to me but I ignored him.

In the kitchen, Mrs. Brier was slamming things around. She glared at me when I walked in.

"Go ahead and give me dirty looks," I said as I picked up Bear's pan and filled it with dog food. "If you think this war is over, you'd better think again. I'm going to make you sorry if it's the last thing I ever do."

"I won't stand for you speaking to me like that," she said. Her eyes were practically bulging.

"What are you going to do about it, tattle on me?" I asked. I put Bear's pan down and watched her gobble up her food.

"Dr. Carver won't put up with your attitude, missy," Mrs. Brier said.

I stared at her. "He never does anything, no matter what happens. That's why *you're* still here. He's not going to do anything about me, either. But if you ever cause any harm to Bear again, I'll make sure everybody finds out. There won't be anybody in Fox Crossing who doesn't know you tried to kill my dog."

She tried to answer me back, but I covered both my ears and started humming. I could tell by her face that she was crazy—mad, and I was glad. I wanted her to be upset. I wanted her to quit, since Will was too lazy or indifferent or uncaring to fire her.

I wanted to make trouble!

When she served dinner, I filled my plate and took it up to my room. Nobody argued with me. Every time anyone tried to talk to me, I shouted, "Leave me alone! I don't care about you!"

Tracey wasn't at the table, so I supposed that I'd hurt her feelings, and I didn't care about that, either.

Around eight o'clock, I heard Tracey go downstairs. The door to the den shut, which was unusual. A few minutes later, Mrs. Brier left the house. I toyed with the idea of going down and trying to have a meaningful conversation with Mom, Will, and Tracey, but gave that idea up in a hurry. They weren't any more likely to understand my concern for Bear now than they were earlier in the day.

I gave them time to get involved in one of their stupid

word games, and then I called Paige on the upstairs phone.

She didn't sound especially glad to hear my voice, but I was so upset that I leaped into my story about Bear and Mrs. Brier. When I finished, Paige sighed.

"You ought to give the puppy back to Thad," she said, sounding exasperated. "It makes me sick to hear about things like that. I'll bet he's been expecting something else to go wrong."

"I can't give her back because I love her too much," I said, and I began crying. She wasn't at all sympathetic with me and I couldn't understand why. "Everything would be all right if it weren't for Mrs. Brier."

"She's going to be there until the end of time," Paige said sharply. "Why don't you face up to it?"

I had a hard time answering her for a moment. She was right. But what I couldn't understand was why she sounded so angry. "What's wrong, Paige? Are you mad at me about something?"

"I'm sick of hearing about Bear, that's all," she said. "If things are really that bad there, why you don't do something? I mean, Heather, if Bear was practically dead from the cold, like you said, why are you even thinking of exposing her to Mrs. Brier again tomorrow?"

Her voice was so sharp that I cringed. "Well, maybe she wasn't practically dead," I said. "I guess I exaggerated a little. But she was soaked and cold and scared. Mrs. Brier was mean, Paige. She really was."

"Give the dog back."

"Paige, what's wrong?" I cried.

She didn't say anything for a moment, then she sighed again and said, "Thad told me this afternoon that Colin asked you to go to the Thanksgiving dance while the two of you were at my party."

"I'm not going," I said quickly. "I told him that."

"Why didn't you tell me that he'd asked you? Why

did you let me go on and on about how much I wanted him to ask me? You should have told me, Heather. Friends talk to each other. They don't keep secrets, especially ones like that.''

And then, before I could say another word, she hung up on me.

I sat there, stunned, holding the telephone.

Darn Colin anyway! I slammed down the phone and was going to my room, but changed my mind and called Colin instead.

He answered the phone. ''You've got a lot of nerve!'' I shouted at him. ''You had to go and blab that you'd asked me to the dance!''

''Thad told you?'' he cried. ''Did he happen to mention that I'd told him *before* you asked me not to say anything?''

''Thad didn't tell me,'' I said in a low, angry voice. ''Paige told me. And she's so upset with me that she hung up on me.''

I could hear Colin breathing on the line. Then he said bewilderedly, ''What's she got to be upset about?''

''You are an absolutely incredible jerk,'' I said, and I hung up on him.

Wonderful, I thought. If I keep this up, I not only won't have a family in Fox Crossing, but I won't have a friend, either.

I went to bed and listened to Bear snore. Later, much later, I heard Tracey come upstairs.

Good old absentminded Tracey, I thought bitterly. So busy talking on the phone that she forgot all about the pup.

And why was she calling her dad anyway? Whatever she was talking to him about could have waited until he got home tonight.

I was too upset to sleep. Long after midnight, I heard

Tracey in the bathroom between our bedrooms, taking a shower.

An hour later she was back in the bathroom again, running water into a glass.

And an hour later, she was getting another drink of water.

Good, I thought meanly. I was glad that I wasn't the only one in the house who couldn't sleep that night.

Chapter 10

Thought for the day: People who use obscene language are demonstrating their ignorance. An intelligent person can always find a respectable word that is just as offensive.

Harold Z. Zoppler, Principal
Fox Crossing High School

The next morning I got up earlier than usual, and by the time Mrs. Brier showed up, I had fed Bear and taken her for a quick walk around the block. Mrs. Brier looked subdued for once, and when I walked through the kitchen with the puppy, she didn't say anything or even give us a dirty look.

I didn't take the credit for her attitude, though. Will probably had said something to her the night before.

Mom was coming downstairs as I was going up. "I'm leaving for school now," I said. "Please put Bear in my room before you leave for the clinic this afternoon. I'll be home as soon as I can."

"Just a minute, Heather," Mom said, and she looked quickly back over her shoulder. "There's something you need to know. We would have told you last night but—"

"Gotta run, Mom," I said, and I hurried past her. I didn't care what she had to tell me. Bear and I had to survive in that house, and we weren't going to manage it if I listened to all the explanations and excuses everybody else invented for everything.

I could hear Tracey in the bathroom, but I didn't call out good morning to her the way I usually did. And I wasn't going to wait and walk to school with her, either. Instead, I grabbed up my books and ran back down the stairs.

"Heather?" Will called out from the direction of the kitchen.

For an answer, I slammed the front door.

My attitude was scaring even me. The only other person I'd ever heard of who behaved like such a brat was my cousin Erin. According to Aunt Ellen, Erin had once been suspended from her school in Oregon for all sorts of awful behavior that began after her parents were killed in an accident.

I didn't have a nightmare reason like that for acting up, and I certainly wasn't going to make that sort of trouble for myself at school. But I considered Bear's welfare important. Somehow or other, those people who thought of themselves as my family were going to face up to just exactly how rotten Mrs. Brier was.

School wasn't going to be an escape for me, though. I had the problem Colin caused me with Paige, too, and I had no idea how I was going to fix it.

I got to school so early that hardly anyone was there. Sandy, still half-asleep, was combing out her hair in the john nearest my locker.

"Don't say good morning to me, Heather," she said. "It's not good and it can't really be morning." She yawned hugely and leaned against the counter under the mirror. "Can you believe how ugly I am?"

"No, because my own face stops trucks and cracks mirrors," I said. "But I've got so many other troubles that being hideous doesn't matter very much." I told her what had happened with Bear and then what had happened between Paige and me.

Sandy gaped at me. "But that's awful! Poor Bear.

And poor Paige. You know how crazy she is about Colin. Gee, I wish you'd told her right away that he asked you to the dance.''

"I should have. I'm not just exceedingly ugly—I'm also exceedingly stupid. I thought if I turned him down and warned him not to tell anybody that he'd asked me, everything would be okay.''

"You're kidding,'' she said glumly. "Around this school, there's no such thing as a secret. I'll bet the first thing he did after he asked you was go tell Thad so that Thad wouldn't ask you. What are you going to do?''

"About what? Bear or Paige? I'm hoping that Mrs. Brier drops dead, but since that isn't likely to happen, I'm acting like a class-A monster and trying to shake everybody up about the dog.''

"Lots of luck with that one,'' Sandy said. "The last time I tried to make a point that way, my dad gave me a dollar bill and told me he'd give me another if I took my little brother and ran away from home.''

I laughed. "He sounds like my Uncle Jock. Or Paige's dad.''

"Meanwhile, how are you safeguarding the puppy? You know how angry Thad would be if he heard about this.''

"Don't tell him!'' I said. "Mom will leave Bear in my room in the afternoon, so Mrs. Brier won't have an excuse to even see the dog. And I won't be letting her out of my sight when I'm home.''

"Hmm,'' Sandy said doubtfully. "What about Paige?''

"I tried explaining to her last night on the phone, but she wasn't impressed. I'll try again.''

"Fat lot of good that's going to do,'' Sandy said. "She's probably hurt because you didn't tell her, but she's also hurt that Colin isn't crazy about her. I would be.''

"What should I do?" I asked, but before Sandy could answer, Paige came in, took a quick look at me, and left.

I ran after her, but she wouldn't wait for me, and there were a zillion people in the hall staring at us. I crept back into the john with Sandy.

"She didn't look too happy," Sandy said.

"No. And did you notice that she's wearing her hair different?" I looked at myself in the mirror and bit my lip. "She's brushed back her bangs and parted her hair on the side."

"We won't have any trouble telling the two of you apart now," Sandy said. She tucked her shirt snugly inside her belt and picked up her books, then looked at me again. "Especially since you look so weird. Since when did you start wearing one white sock and one yellow?"

I looked down and groaned. "I don't believe I did that."

"Tell everybody that you did it on purpose," Sandy advised. "That's what I did when I wore my sweater inside out."

My laugh was a pretty weak one.

Paige managed to escape walking with me between classes, no matter how hard I tried to catch up with her. And while I was trying to catch her, Colin was trying to catch me.

"Leave me alone," I said to him finally. "Haven't you caused me enough trouble?"

He shrugged helplessly. "I only wanted to tell you how sorry I am. Gee, give a guy a chance."

"No!" I said. "If Paige sees us talking together, she'll get the wrong idea."

"Paige? Why should she?"

I considered socking him and changed my mind. Mr. Stark was standing halfway down the hall, watching us.

"You must have the thickest skull in town," I told Colin. "Don't you know that Paige likes you?"

He shrugged again. "I like her, too," he said. "She's a great pal."

"Oh, you idiot," I growled, and I walked away from him. Hopeless.

Tracey smiled lifelessly at me when I saw her outside the school library, but I looked away. She wasn't getting off the hook yet.

Micky and I shared my homemade lunch while we sat at Thad's table, but Thad spent the whole lunch break discussing his father's car with two other boys. Well, I consoled myself, at least he didn't bring up Colin and Paige to me. Or Bear. I didn't see Paige in the cafeteria, and Sandy told us later that Paige had been in the student lounge.

The day didn't get any better as it progressed. Between my last two classes, I saw Mom and Will coming out of Mr. Stark's office. For a moment, I was so stunned that I stopped dead. Then I ran after them, on the verge of calling out to them.

But I stopped again. What if Mr. Stark had asked them to school to talk about me? Had he been brooding about that cat business in the cafeteria? I still wasn't allowed to buy my lunch—not that I wanted to. And I had more or less reformed as far as practical jokes were concerned. But Mr. Stark spent an awful lot of time watching me. Well, he watched Paige, too. And a few of the other sophomores.

Actually, he watched practically everybody. No, Mom and Will weren't at school because of me.

But why, then?

I expected to find them at home when I got there at three, but the house was empty except for Mrs. Brier and Bear. Bear was asleep on my bed, and Mrs. Brier was knocking the bottoms out of a couple of pans in the kitchen.

I shoved open the kitchen door. "Where's my mother?" I demanded.

"How should I know?" she snapped back.

I went back upstairs to wait. After a while Tracey came home, but I still didn't want to talk to her, so I ignored her when she rapped on my door. I took Bear for a walk, stopped by Micky's house for a few minutes, and got home just as Mom and Will drove up in front.

We all looked at each other soberly. "I saw you at school today," I said. "Did it have something to do with me?"

"No," Mom said. "We've been trying to tell you something."

"About what?"

"Come inside," Will said.

I followed them inside and sat down in the den with them.

"Tracey is losing her college scholarship," Will said quietly. "She's been accused of plagiarizing the essay she wrote."

"What?" I asked stupidly. "What?" Tracey was accused of cheating? I couldn't believe it.

Will repeated himself. "We've been very upset about this and wanted to talk to you about it last night, but things didn't seem to work out very well."

That was an understatement. "I'm sorry," I said. "But I was upset, too."

"Yes, we understand that," Mom said, "but we've tried to handle the problem with the puppy as best we could. Now we have to concentrate on supporting Tracey."

I nodded and sat back to listen while they explained that Mr. Stark had been given a quarterly magazine that contained an article almost exactly like the essay Tracey wrote. He had no choice but to tell the organization that awarded the scholarship.

"Are you sure the article was almost the same?" I asked. "Did you see it?"

Mom took several folded sheets of paper out of her purse and handed them to me. "This is a photocopy of it. You read Tracey's essay, didn't you?" When I nodded, she said, "You'll see that they're almost exactly the same, then."

"I don't know how this happened," Will said. "Tracey wouldn't plagiarize. It must be some kind of coincidence, but no one will believe that."

"Mr. Stark certainly won't," I grumbled as I read the article.

"Actually, he's as upset as we are," Will said. "But he was presented with the original of this and showed it to us today. There's no mistake that the article actually appeared in the quarterly."

I put the papers down. "Who gave him the quarterly?" I asked. "One of the teachers?"

"No, it came from one of the seniors who is also interested in archaeology."

"Who?" I asked.

Will sighed. "Her name is Kix Michaels."

I snorted in disgust. "I don't think that Kix Michaels is interested in anything except Darren Pauley."

And then something clicked.

"Darren Pauley wanted that scholarship," I told Mom and Will.

"Well, he'll get it now," Will said. "He was the runner-up."

"I'll bet Darren and Kix are telling everybody," I said bitterly. No matter what problems we had at home, I couldn't bear the thought of Tracey being disgraced at school.

"There isn't much anyone can do about that," Mom said.

"How's Tracey taking it?" I asked.

Mom looked at Will, and he said, "She keeps her feelings to herself."

Yes, I thought. And maybe she'd be better off if she screamed and banged her head against the wall.

"Is there anything I can do?" I asked.

"We wish you wouldn't blame her for problems with the puppy," Mom said. "Tracey was late yesterday because she had called Will and wanted to see him for a few minutes after school. She didn't know that Mrs. Brier was going out."

I sighed. "I shouldn't have blamed Tracey, then. But that still doesn't excuse Mrs. Brier putting Bear out in the rain and leaving her there."

"It won't happen again," Will said. "I've made certain of that."

Sure you have, I thought as I went upstairs to my room. Maybe Mrs. Brier won't leave Bear outside in bad weather, but she'll think up something else to do to Bear and me.

After dinner, I got a phone call from Thad. The shock almost left me unconscious on the hall floor.

"How's Bear getting along?" he said. "I meant to ask you at school today."

"Has somebody been talking to you?" I cried.

"About what? What's wrong? Has something happened to Bear?" He sounded surprised—and more than a little agitated.

"Bear is chewing on the leg of the table right at this moment," I said and I bent to push her away from her new toy. "So I'd say she's feeling completely herself." I wasn't about to bring up the day before and the storm if he didn't already know.

"Good," he said. "I don't mean that she's chewing on the table. I mean good that . . ."

"I understand," I said. I understood perfectly that the only reason he was talking to me on the phone was the dog. "Thanks for asking about her. Good-bye."

"Wait!" he shouted.

"Yes?" I asked. Now what?

There was a small silence, and then he blurted, "I heard that you're not going to the dance with Colin."

"People gossip too much," I said, and my voice must have been sharper than I'd intended, because Thad apologized for bothering me, said good-bye, and hung up.

Why didn't anything ever go right?

I wrote Amelia a long letter that night, telling her everything and adding a line expressing my urgent wish that I'd never been born.

Chapter 11

When things aren't going right, every day is a year long and a week drags into eternity. The whole school found out about Tracey so fast that I wouldn't have been surprised to see Darren and Kix passing out leaflets in the halls between classes. You could tell, though, that quiet Tracey was really admired, because everybody's sympathy was with her. Darren, who never had been surrounded by crowds of hysterical admirers, smirked a lot, but he did it all by himself. Everybody except Kix avoided him.

However, sympathy didn't change anything for Tracey. She marched through her school days just like she always did. I don't suppose Mom and Will knew, though, that she didn't sleep well. I heard her moving around in her room for hours every night.

Besides Darren and Kix, there was one other person who was glad that Tracey was in trouble. As soon as Mrs. Brier found out, she cheered up and went around the house humming to herself. I even caught her smiling at Bear. Bear thought Mrs. Brier was snarling, however, and she yelped and got out of her way.

100

The housekeeper's change of mood puzzled me.

"How come Mrs. Brier doesn't feel bad about Tracey?" I asked Mom one evening when I had a minute alone with her.

"What makes you think she doesn't?" Mom asked, surprised. She was fixing a late snack for us in the kitchen, but she stopped spooning applesauce over gingerbread and stared at me.

"She's sure been happy the last few days." I folded paper napkins and put them on the tray. "She doesn't exactly talk to me, but she's stopped yelling every time I walk in the door. I thought Tracey was her favorite person in the whole universe."

"She is," Mom said thoughtfully. "Maybe Mrs. Brier's just trying to distract Tracey. She seemed genuinely upset when we told her about the scholarship."

"If she is, she's sure doing a good job of hiding it."

Tracey came in, then, to help us carry the dessert and hot chocolate to the den, so we couldn't go on with the conversation, but I began watching Mrs. Brier closely after that. She was up to something.

At school, Paige seemed to be lost to me as a friend. Oh, she spoke to me, occasionally and briefly, but I never saw her after school. The days of "Paige One" and "Paige Two" and "Double Trouble" were over. With Paige's new hairstyle, not many people had problems telling us apart any longer. I missed her. We'd almost been best friends. But I couldn't help being angry, too. I wished that she'd given me a chance—or tried to imagine how she would have felt in my place.

Sandy, Micky, and I got together several times a week, though, sometimes at my house and sometimes at theirs.

One afternoon, when a fresh snow had fallen, we took Bear for a walk in the park and ran into Colin and Thad. Bear recognized Thad and galloped up to him.

He knelt in the snow and hugged her. "She's not exactly graceful, is she?" he said, laughing. "When I first saw you, I thought you were walking a baby buffalo. How's she getting along? At home, I mean?"

"That's the only thing you ever ask me," I said. "Bear's fine. I think Mrs. Brier is beginning to like her."

"You're kidding," Colin said. "Mrs. Brier doesn't look like she knows how to like anything or anybody."

"She likes Tracey," Micky said. "We all know that."

Everybody looked embarrassed suddenly.

"Poor Tracey," Sandy said. "Every time I think about what happened to her, I get sick all over."

"What exactly did happen?" Colin asked. "It's hard to believe that she would have copied something out of a magazine. First, she's smart enough to write her own stuff. And even if she wasn't, only a moron would copy something out of a magazine that anybody could read."

"Well, it's not exactly a monthly magazine," I said. "It's a quarterly, and only the people who belong to the Pearsoll Society get copies. Well, libraries do. But you wouldn't find a copy at the mall."

"But still," Colin protested, "I don't believe she did it."

No one else did, either, but no one had an explanation.

"Have you seen this quarterly?" Thad asked.

We'd started walking again, and Bear insisted on lumbering along next to Thad. I gave up hauling on her leash and just handed it to him.

"I looked for it in the school library, but the librarian said they didn't have it," I said. "I'm going to try the public library after dinner this evening."

"Let's do it now," Colin said.

"I've got Bear. They won't let her in," I told him.

"I'll walk Bear around the block while you guys go in and look," Thad said.

The library was only four blocks away, and Bear was more than glad to spend time with Thad, so the rest of us hurried off.

The librarian told us that they had copies of the Pearsoll Society quarterly, but we couldn't check them out because they were reference material. The particular issue we were interested in wasn't available, though.

"How come?" I asked. "I thought you wouldn't let anyone check them out."

She shrugged. "It's been misplaced. Or stolen. Unfortunately, reference material disappears sometimes. Would you like to see some of the other issues?"

"Yes," Micky said firmly.

When the librarian went to get them, Micky whispered, "We might as well find out what they're like."

"What for?" Colin asked. "If we can't see the one that's supposed to have the article Tracey copied, who cares what the rest of them look like?"

"I want to see them, too," I said. "Mom showed me the photocopy of the article—and it didn't look like it came from much of a magazine. The print looked like the bulletins we get at school."

"You mean maybe it was done on a computer?" Colin asked.

I shrugged. "I don't know. It didn't look like it was typed, exactly. I can't explain it."

The librarian was back, and she handed Micky several copies of a thin magazine with a shiny cover. We sat at a nearby table and Micky passed out the magazines.

There were no pictures in mine, not even on the slick cover. Inside, the pages were printed on paper that looked and felt like typing paper. The whole thing was stapled together.

"This looks practically homemade," Sandy said.

"It looks like the stuff my dad brings home from work," Micky said. "It's done on a computer that has some sort of publishing software. I bet Thad would know about it. Or his dad. His dad has a computer and all kinds of junk he fools around with."

She jumped up. "I'll go trade places with Thad and let him come in and look at this."

I turned the pages of my copy of the quarterly. "If the people who put this out could do it all with a computer, then so could somebody else who had the right equipment." I looked up at my friends. "Are you thinking what I'm thinking?"

"I'm afraid to say it out loud because it would sound so dumb," Sandy said.

"I'll say it," I said. "What was to stop Kix from giving Mr. Stark a copy that she faked?"

But Colin shook his head. "Somebody could fake the inside, but what about the cover? It looks professional. The Pearsoll Society might do the inside themselves, but they have the covers done by a professional printer."

Sandy rubbed her finger over the library stamp on the cover. "Look, the ink comes right off this slick paper."

"Kix could have stolen the missing copy," I said, barely able to breathe. "And rubbed the stamp off the cover and used it."

"I'm going to get Thad," Micky said, and she ran out of the library.

"We need to find a copy of the missing quarterly," I said. "But not the one that Mr. Stark has."

"Right. We need one that Kix and Darren couldn't have fooled around with," Colin said.

"Maybe there's a copy at the college library," I said.

"We can't check out stuff from there," Sandy said. "We aren't students."

"Thad's parents work there," I said. "He could ask

them to bring one home. Then we could check to see if that article Mom has a copy of is really in it."

"And if it isn't . . ." Colin said.

"Then we'll know that Kix substituted one of her own to show Mr. Stark." I leaned back in my chair and grinned.

But Sandy shook her head. "Kix isn't smart enough to write an article that would fool Mr. Stark."

I groaned. "Right."

"But Darren might be," Colin said. "He could have taken Tracey's and changed a few things here and there."

"And then found somebody who knew how to duplicate the style of the quarterly." I was suddenly excited, and absolutely certain I was right. "We've got to find the real one."

Thad came in then, his blond hair tousled from the wind. "What's up, you guys? Micky says you're onto something."

Colin told him quickly and showed him one of the quarterlies. "Could your dad print something like this?"

"Sure." Thad thumbed through the magazine. "This isn't hard. But he couldn't do the cover. That's a professional printing job, and an expensive one, too, I bet."

"We aren't worried about the cover," I said. "We know how they got that, don't we?"

And the others at the table nodded.

We left the library, found Micky and Bear, and everybody walked Bear and me home. I could tell by the cars in the driveway that both Mom and Will were home, and my first impulse was to run in and tell them everything.

I decided, though, that it would be better to find proof first. There was no point in getting everybody's hopes up. If we were wrong—and we could be—then everybody would be more disappointed than ever. And I'd look like a trouble-making idiot again to my family. But all through dinner, I had to work really hard to keep my mouth shut.

If everything turns out right, I told myself, I'm going to give them the biggest surprise they've ever had. And maybe, finally, everybody would loosen up and be real for a change. Maybe they'd appreciate my friends and me. If I did something right for a change, the Carvers—including my mother—would see me as something more than a noisy pest.

I replayed a variation of my favorite fantasy, which had grown a little ragged around the edges. Each day when we all got home, we'd share ideas and good times and bad times. At dinner, we'd talk to each other, laughing and debating and telling each other about things that really mattered. We'd care about each other so that the whole world could see. And we'd be safe and happy—and a real family. End of fantasy.

In real life, we ate in almost complete silence, as usual, then went to the den for dessert and listened to music while Mom and Will shared the newspaper and Tracey and I played a half-hearted game of Scrabble. Tracey sighed a lot.

From the kitchen we heard a restrained clang of pots and pans. Mrs. Brier was still riding high on a tide of delirious joy, for some reason.

My good mood vanished. Probably I was wrong about the quarterly and Kix substituting another article. It was too farfetched. Thad would ask his parents to bring home a copy and it would be exactly the same as the one Kix had given Mr. Stark.

Hadn't I learned how hopeless fantasies can be?

Chapter 12

Thought for the day: We are the total of everything
that has ever happened to us. And more things have
happened to some people than to others.

Harold Z. Zoppler, Principal
Fox Crossing High School

My cousin Amelia had written once suggesting that
maybe I was expecting too much by wanting my new
family to be exactly like all my fantasies. But she said
that she admired me tremendously, however, because I
was able to put other people ahead of myself when it
really mattered. That was only true part of the time, but
I actually did forget about horrible Mrs. Brier for hours
on end while my friends and I tried to help Tracey by
untangling the mystery of the plagiarized essay.

During lunch break in the cafeteria the next day,
Sandy said that other people might be wondering, too,
if Kix and Darren were responsible for what had
happened to Tracey.

"It's obvious to us, but probably not to the grown-
ups who don't have to deal with them when they're being their everyday obnoxious selves," Micky said. "I'll
bet there isn't a student in this school who doesn't hate
them. But how do we figure out exactly what happened?" She stirred the food on her plate suspiciously.
"I wish my mother didn't have this weird idea that I'll
die if I don't eat a hot lunch. Heather, how much longer
do you have to wait before you buy food here again?"

"Until the end of the semester," I said, and I took a bite of my peanut butter and sliced apple sandwich. "But I won't buy anything then, either. Since I discovered what great lunches I pack myself, I'm not getting involved in the generation gap again."

"What generation gap?" Thad asked. He apparently didn't have taste buds, because he'd just brought back his second helping of the unidentifiable casserole that was the day's special.

"The big gap that yawns between the adults who plan school lunches and the poor saps who buy them," I said. I'd also brought a sizable chunk of gingerbread from home, which I had no intention of sharing. "Thad, can you call your parents at college and ask them if they've looked in the library yet for that quarterly? I don't know if I can wait until tonight."

"I can call," Thad said reluctantly, "but then they'd want to know what the big hurry is, and if I tell them, they'd skid right in to Dr. Carver and blab everything. I thought we were going to keep our plans a secret until we can prove that Tracey didn't do anything. You know that parents can't keep secrets."

"Right," I groaned. "But they won't forget about looking for the quarterly, will they?"

Thad laughed his soft, husky laugh. "No way. They think I've developed a sudden interest in archaeology and they're already planning where I'll do my graduate work."

Colin, eating a brownie, choked a little. "I can see that you haven't told them about your new career intentions. Thad Shipton, incredibly famous international spy."

Thad laughed again, and I got a sudden case of goose bumps. A few weeks before, I had daydreamed occasionally about going out with Thad on a double date with Paige and Colin. Daydreamed *occasionally?* I'm kidding, of course. It crossed my mind every time I saw Thad. Well, that was over, along with all the rest of my homegrown fairy tales, but I couldn't help thinking again that they were two of the nicest boys I'd ever known. Unfortunately, the wrong one wanted to take me out and neither of them seemed to care about Paige except as a pal.

"I may need all the spies I can get," I told them. "If we're right, and somehow Kix and Darren faked part of the quarterly, we'll still have to find out who did the actual printing."

"Anybody with a computer at home and the right software," Thad said.

"Does Darren have a computer? Or Kix?" I asked.

"Lots of people have 'em," Colin said.

"We only play games on ours," Micky said. "I bet that's what most people use them for."

"That's not all the computer club kids use theirs for," Thad said, "but I've never seen Darren hanging around with them, so he might not be interested."

"Who would know if Darren and Kix have computers?" I asked. I'd finished my lunch, so I wadded up my paper bag and threw it inexpertly toward the trash can. Missed.

"Pig," Thad said to me cheerfully, and then he went on with our conversation. "If Darren and Kix have computers, their friends would know."

"What friends?" Sandy snickered. "They haven't got any."

"Everybody has friends," Thad said, and he threw his arm around Sandy's shoulder. I'd been picking up my garbage, and the sight of Thad hugging Sandy bothered me so much that I couldn't stand to watch, so I pretended a big interest in what I was doing.

"Why are you looking in the trash bin?" Colin asked me.

I sighed. "No reason." Thad wasn't hugging Sandy anymore and I didn't die of jealousy after all. The moment passed, and no one had paid any attention to it but me.

We left the cafeteria in a group and Paige caught up with Sandy and Micky in the hall, but she didn't say anything to me. She didn't talk to Colin, either, and he seemed embarrassed by her presence. I guess he'd finally figured out what I meant when I told him about Paige. The more time that passed, the harder it was for me to believe what good friends Paige and I had been. One stupid little secret had changed everything. Now I was keeping a bigger one from her—but she might not care about what had happened to Tracey.

Tracey walked home from school with me that afternoon. We were going our own ways more and more, so I was surprised when I found her waiting for me outside the school door.

I remembered the unfinished conversation I'd had at lunch about Darren and Kix. This seemed as good an opportunity as any to learn a few things about them. But I had to be careful and not give Tracey any reason to wonder why I was curious about them.

"How come you don't have a computer?" I asked her. "Lots of kids do."

"I'm not interested in them," she said. "Do you want one?"

"Not particularly." The sidewalk was icy in places, so we were walking slowly, watching where we stepped. I hoped there was nothing in my expression to give me away. "Most of the really smart kids in school like computers."

"I suppose," Tracey said.

I named off some of her friends and asked if they used computers. Some did and some didn't.

"That Darren, he looks like the sort who'd be a hacker

and break into secret government computer systems." I glanced up quickly at Tracey's face.

Her expression didn't tell me anything. "I've never really known him very well."

"But you've gone all through school with him, haven't you?" I asked.

"I don't have room for people like him in my life," Tracey said abruptly.

I didn't learn anything about Darren, but I confirmed something I'd suspected about my stepsister. Control was so important to her that if she didn't like someone, she wouldn't even allow herself to be curious about him. It was as if that person didn't exist.

I thought of the times when I'd been angry with people and couldn't stop thinking about them. Tracey didn't waste time like that, and for about thirty seconds I wished I could be like her.

No, I decided, I'd rather go on the way I was. Maybe I had more ups and downs than Tracey, but at least I could feel something. Tracey was losing her college scholarship, which meant more to her than anything else. Yet to look at her you wouldn't think that the loss mattered much more than losing a book.

But, still, I heard her getting up over and over in the middle of the night, so the private Tracey was upset even though the public one marched on through life like a robot.

Half an hour later I overheard a conversation that gave me something new to wonder about. I'd put Bear on a leash and taken her out the front door, got half a block and remembered that I wanted to mail a letter to Amelia, so I went back for it.

I guess Mrs. Brier didn't hear me open the door. "You're going to be glad about this someday," she was saying.

Was she talking on the phone? I couldn't imagine her

caring whether or not anybody was glad about anything, so I stopped to listen.

"You'll be much better off at home, going to college where your father teaches," Mrs. Brier said.

She was talking to Tracey in the den, but Tracey wasn't responding.

"Maybe losing that scholarship will turn out to be the best thing that ever happened to you," Mrs. Brier said. "Who knows what might have gone wrong on the other side of the country when you were with strangers. Maybe you're being spared something awful."

"Whatever," Tracey said. She didn't sound rude or annoyed. She sounded cold. "Are we going to have rice for dinner or potatoes?" she asked abruptly.

I grabbed up my letter from the hall table and led Bear back outside. Good grief. If someone had said to me what Mrs. Brier had just said to Tracey, I would have blown up.

And if all this scholarship mess had happened to Amelia, she would have exploded, too. There wouldn't have been a quiet meeting with the principal, there would have been a riot. She would have stomped all over town banging on doors until she found out everything there was to know about the article in that quarterly. Maybe she couldn't have proved anything, but she would have made a few people nervous.

"I don't believe Tracey," I said aloud. "She can't be real." Bear looked back at me and wagged her tail.

I wished that I could understand my stepsister. There had to be an explanation for the way she cut herself off from feeling anything.

Bear and I went home. Thad said he'd call as soon as his parents brought home the quarterly, and I found myself watching the clock impatiently. Will came in and Mom arrived ten minutes later. Mrs. Brier clomped into the den and told us that dinner was ready.

The phone rang.

"It's for me, I think," I called out as I ran to answer it.

"Heather?" Thad said. "I've got some strange news. That issue of the magazine is missing from the college library, too."

"Are your parents sure?" I asked.

"Yes. It looks like the person who took the one from the public library dropped by the college, too."

"But only college students can check out books and magazines there," I said.

"I know," Thad said. "But somebody managed it."

I bit my lip. "Now what do we do?"

"Look somewhere else," Thad said. "There's the county library, out past Abbey Falls, and it's open tonight. Would you like to drive out there with me?"

Before I could answer, Thad went on to tell me that he'd asked his dad for a sample page of different printing styles. "It's pretty interesting," he said. "I'll bring it along and show you."

"You didn't tell him why you wanted it, did you?" I asked.

"No. I'd told him before that my English class wants to print some of the short stories the kids have written. He thinks I'm working on that idea. Heather, listen. One of the lines on Dad's page looks like the print in the quarterlies we saw in the public library. In case the county library doesn't have one, will you bring along the copy of that article so we can see if I'm right?"

"I don't know if I can get it," I said, lowering my voice. "I'll try though."

"Good. I'll pick you up at seven. Is that all right?"

"Sure. See you then." When I hung up, I held my hand on the phone for a moment, savoring the feelings I had. Maybe Thad had forgiven me for bringing Bear into Mrs. Brier's reach.

Unfortunately, though, I had just created another opportunity to look rude, stupid, and generally unfit to be a member of the Carver household. When I walked into the dining room late, everybody was politely waiting for me—in total silence.

"Ah, Heather," Will said calmly.

Mrs. Brier served the food—and an especially nasty smirk intended for me. While we ate, I explained that I was going to the county library after dinner.

"Will someone be home, or should I take Bear with me?" I asked.

"It's a school night," Tracey said. "I'll be here."

"So will we," Mom said. "Bear's in good hands."

Mom must have known that Mrs. Brier was standing right behind her. Did I detect a small and slightly nasty smile on Mom's face?

I did.

Will didn't notice anything and neither did Tracey, but Mrs. Brier knew exactly what Mom had on her mind when she said that.

I smiled broadly at Mrs. Brier and she rushed out of the room. Five seconds later pans clanged in the sink.

Mom looked at me innocently. "Would you like butter for your roll, Heather?" she asked.

I shook my head, struggling to keep from laughing. We ate the rest of our meal in silence except for Will's mild observation that he was arranging for someone to come to the house to clean the leaves out of the gutters.

I could barely contain my excitement at that amazing news.

Thad came promptly at seven. I kissed Bear good-bye and hurried out. I'd taken the article out of the desk in the den and hidden it in my notebook, and I felt so guilty that I was afraid it would drop on the floor in front of everybody. There was no way I could ever even think of being a successful shoplifter.

In the car, Thad asked, "Did you get it?"

"Yes," I said, pulling it out. "I hate feeling like a thief, though."

"Don't," Thad said. "You're doing this for Tracey."

He drove the car a few blocks and stopped in the parking lot of a fast food restaurant. "This is what my dad ran on his printer," he said. He turned on the car's interior light and handed me the page.

In a dozen different print styles, I read the words, "Thad, clean out the garage."

Without meaning to, I laughed aloud.

"Get serious," Thad said. "Look at the fourth line down. Doesn't that look like the print in the quarterlies?"

I held out the photocopy of the article that Mr. Stark had given Mom and Will. Thad bent over it, examining it first and then the page he held.

"They're exactly the same," he said, "except that I think my dad's print is a little darker."

I leaned back in my seat. "Now all we have to do is see if this is really the article that was in that issue of the quarterly or if somebody substituted it for the real one."

"And the real one would be completely different from Tracey's," Thad said excitedly, "and prove that she was set up."

"Let's go to the library," I said. "Maybe we can clear everything up tonight."

Thad pulled me close in a quick hug and kissed my cheek. "Here we go."

All the way there I was caught up in a new fantasy, a new wonderful daydream where I proved that Tracey hadn't cheated, she got her scholarship back, and everybody in the family became not only grateful for what I'd done, but also learned to be warm and openly caring and less formal.

"There's the library." Thad pulled into the parking lot. "It could all be over in ten minutes," he said.

"Let's go." Ten minutes wasn't long to wait for the beginning of lots of good things, and I was so excited that my hands were shaking.

Thad was almost right. It was over in less than ten minutes because the library didn't have any copies of the *Pearsoll Society Quarterly*.

Neither of us had much to say on the way home. I was too disappointed to talk about the problem. And I had a new worry. Now that this trip was over, there wasn't a reason for Thad to take me anywhere else.

It was barely eight o'clock when we stopped in front of my house. I turned in my seat and smiled my best smile, knowing that he probably couldn't see it in the dark. But I wanted my voice to sound as if I was smiling.

"Thanks for trying," I told Thad. "I appreciate everything you've done, believe me."

"I could see how worried you were about Tracey," he said. "I know you don't like living here, and you're probably not very happy with the Carvers either. But you've been . . ." He stopped talking.

"Been what?" I asked nervously.

"Great," he said. "Really nice in spite of being so . . ."

"So *what?*" I asked, dumbfounded.

"Stubborn," he said, and he bent his head quickly and kissed me.

And then, before I had a chance to do or say anything, he opened his car door, trotted around and opened mine and said, "I'll walk you to the door."

"The porch light is on," I said stupidly. "I can see the steps just fine."

"Okay," he said. "See you tomorrow then."

When I got to my front door, I looked back and waved. What did he mean by calling me stubborn?

I went inside, thoroughly discouraged because the trip hadn't been successful. There had been a time when getting kissed good night by Thad Shipton would have left me nearly half-witted with delight. Now I had other things on my mind.

"Is that you, Heather?" Mom called from the den.

"Yes," I called back.

"Did you find what you needed?"

"No," I said. "I'll have to look somewhere else."

"Too bad," Mom called. "Sorry, Heather."

Bear galloped out of the den and followed me upstairs. I sat on the bed with her for a long time, thinking. There had to be a copy of that quarterly somewhere. But where? Would it be possible to write to the society and ask for one? Why not?

Later, after everyone was asleep, I put the article back where I'd found it. Maybe proving that Tracey was innocent would turn out to be hopeless. Or maybe we'd prove it but it would be too late, and that would be awful.

Chapter 13

Thought for the day: Successful students have three things in common. They concentrate and they're persistent. (Pause) That was only two things. Oh, well.

> Harold Z. Zoppler, Principal
> Fox Crossing High School

The next day during lunch, I was thinking about Tracey and barely listening to the conversation going on around me. I'd decided that I would get the address of the Pearsoll Society and write them, asking for a copy of the missing quarterly. Even if I didn't get a reply immediately, I promised myself I wouldn't worry. There was plenty of time—the awards assembly wasn't until February. As long as I could absolutely and completely prove that Tracey was innocent by then, everything would turn out all right.

Sandy, Micky, and some of the other sophomore girls had been talking about the Thanksgiving dance. No one had a date, but they'd been planning what they were going to wear.

I finally tuned in on the conversation. "You're going even if you don't have a date?" I asked. "Is it like a mixer?" The way everyone talked about the dance had given me the idea it was a big event, like the senior prom.

"No, it's not like a mixer," Micky said. "It's much

nicer than that. But only the juniors and seniors date for it."

"Why?" I asked.

They both shrugged. "That's the way it's always been. The juniors and seniors take it more seriously. A lot of parents come to it, too."

"Parents," I marveled. "You mean as chaperones, I guess."

"Some," Sandy admitted. "But most of them just come because it's fun. I guess they get sentimental about ancient times, when they were students here."

"Then it's like a homecoming dance," I said. "Okay, I can see that, but I don't understand why freshmen and sophomores don't even want to have dates."

"Heather," Micky said, "everybody wants a date. We aren't crazy. But you know how it is. The boys won't ask anyone and so we're stuck. Well, some might ask, but they're the ones who go steady."

"Go steady!" Sandy scoffed. "Name one girl in the sophomore class who has a steady boyfriend. Or any kind of boyfriend at all."

Micky shrugged. "You're right. We're boring."

"It's the guys who are boring," Sandy said. "They don't seem to want real dates."

"Just hanging-around type dates," Micky mourned. "This could go on forever, you know."

"I'll bet it's different in Seattle," Sandy said to me. "Did you go out on real dates a lot?"

I had to admit that it wasn't always so different in Seattle.

"But did you ever have a *real* date?" Sandy asked.

I groaned. "I was hoping no one would ever ask about that."

"You did, didn't you?" Micky accused. "Tell us about it."

I shook my head solemnly. "I swore to myself that I

119

would never, never tell what happened. It's too humiliating.''

Sandy looked at Micky. "Can we shake it out of her?"

Micky laughed, but she said, "We'd better not try. It must be a horror story."

"Worse than that," I assured them. "And now if we don't change the subject, I think I'll break out in hives."

"It was that bad?" Micky asked. "Okay, consider the subject changed."

Earlier that day, I'd told them that Thad and I had gone to the county library the night before, but I left out the part about him kissing me. Telling that would spoil it for me because as soon as I didn't have to worry about Tracey, I planned spending some of my spare time wishing it would happen again.

But they hadn't attached any special importance to Thad's taking me to the library. They were still worried about Tracey, however.

"Is Tracey going to the dance?" Sandy asked.

"Sure, as far as I know," I said. "She told me a long time ago that she'd asked John to take her. He did last year, when he was a senior here."

"They've been going together forever," Micky said wistfully. "But if I were her, I don't think I could bring myself to go. I know for an absolute fact that Darren is taking Kix. I heard her telling somebody about her dress. If I were Tracey, I couldn't stand to be in the same room with them."

"They have classes together," I said. "I don't think it bothers her."

"It *must* bother her," Micky said. "It would drive me crazy, knowing that they were responsible for my losing that scholarship—and wondering if they'd plotted against me and laughed at me. And she's got to know that everybody else in the whole school pities her."

Micky looked suddenly uncomfortable. "Maybe people even think that she might have cheated, too, but they don't want to admit it."

"I know," I said. "I've wondered how she stands it. But she just goes on. She's like her father. Neither one of them goes crazy over things like I do."

"Everybody would go crazy over that," Sandy said. "I think they're weird. Oh, sorry, Heather. I didn't mean to put it that way." She looked ready to cry.

"I know what you mean," I said. "I can't get over it myself."

"Doesn't her father care about what happened?" Sandy asked.

"Of course," I told her. "He—and my mom, too— had several talks with Mr. Stark about it. Even Mr. Stark was upset. But he has to tell the scholarship selection committee what happened before anything is formally announced." I offered them the cookies I'd brought from home because I'd lost my appetite.

"Sometimes," I went on slowly, "I think that Will and Tracey don't know how to fix things because they won't let themselves grab on to problems and *make* them turn out right."

Micky cleared her throat, then said quietly, "I told my mother about this. She said that she remembers when Tracey's mother ran away. Once, she said, she saw Tracey all by herself in the park, crying. But when she tried to help her, Tracey ran off."

Appalled, I stared down at the remains of my lunch. Tracey crying in the park, all alone? She'd been such a little girl to have such terrible problems.

In a way, Tracey reminded me of my cousin Erin, whose parents had been killed when she was ten. But Erin's grief and sadness had turned her into a wild little brat who drove her grandparents half crazy—or so Aunt Ellen had told Amelia and me.

That night, while the family was having dessert in the den, Tracey told us that she wasn't going to the dance. No one had asked her about it—I suppose Mom and Will took it for granted that she was still going. She just said simply and quietly that she and John had decided not to go.

"It's probably a good idea," Will said, looking up from his slice of pound cake. "Perhaps we can all go out to dinner that night. With John, of course."

Tracey shrugged. "Sure. I guess." And then she got to her feet and went upstairs.

"I suppose she was afraid of running into Darren and Kix," I said. I desperately wanted to talk about this, to get our feelings out in the open so that we could all grieve for Tracey together.

"Doesn't she see them every day at school?" Mom asked.

"Well, yes, but it would be different at a dance," I said.

"Would it?" Will asked. He seemed genuinely curious.

Couldn't he see how awful it would be to go to something happy like a dance and then be reminded of what those two slugs had done to you?

"I think I see what Heather means," Mom said tactfully. She must have noticed that I was ready to have a stroke.

"Ah," Will said. "Sometimes Tracey reminds me of her grandmother. She was a woman of extraordinary dignity."

I slumped in my chair. Hopeless. Extraordinary dignity? I'd have worried less about Tracey if she had been like a woman of extraordinary temper tantrums. Every time I saw Darren or Kix in the hall, I wanted awfully much to leap on them and bash them into grease spots on the floor.

We went out to dinner the night of the dance. Sandy and Micky begged me to go to the dance with them, but I couldn't see standing around waiting patiently to dance with some boy who didn't have a date either. Also, I knew that Thad wasn't going. He'd mentioned that he and his parents were planning to visit his grandmother in Abbey Falls instead.

On Thanksgiving Day, the Carvers and I had dinner with a professor from the college, his wife, and his four darling little girls. They reminded me so much of my cousins and the happy holidays I'd always spent at Amelia's house that I was too homesick to enjoy the food.

I sure wasn't looking forward to Christmas.

Late on the Sunday evening after Thanksgiving, I got a phone call from Thad. I was really surprised, because I'd heard him making plans with Colin to spend that weekend at the mountain cabin Colin's family had built the summer before.

"Where are you?" I asked as soon as I heard his voice.

"Home," he said. "I just got here. Listen, I've got news. Real news about the quarterly."

"What is it?" I said, automatically lowering my voice in case anyone could hear me.

"Colin and I drove back from the cabin together, and on the way we stopped at the library in Perryville, just in case they might have the quarterly."

"And . . ."

"They had it. We couldn't take it out but we photocopied the whole thing. Every single page."

My heart was beating hard and my ears were ringing. "Did it have the same article in it?"

"No!" Thad said. "It's completely different. You were right all along, Heather. Somebody substituted a different article in the copy that Mr. Stark has."

I pressed the phone against my ear so hard that it hurt. "Are you sure? Really sure?"

"I'd bring it over right now but it's awfully late. Believe me, though, it's different. I'll meet you at school early tomorrow, and you can show it to Mr. Stark. Are you going to tell your family tonight?"

"I want to but I'm too scared," I whispered into the phone. "I know you're sure, but what if you've made a mistake? I need to see it myself, just to be certain."

"Okay. Then I'll see you tomorrow," Thad said. "You can stop worrying now."

"Sure," I said, but I knew I wouldn't get a minute's sleep.

It was hard to go back in the den and sit with Mom and Will without telling them, but I had to see the proof for myself. If I was going to try playing the part of the big hero, I needed to be absolutely certain that I wouldn't end up looking like an idiot.

Tracey had been out with John that evening, and she got home a few minutes later. But she only stuck her head in the door to say hello and tell us that she had homework waiting upstairs for her.

Bear yawned and looked hopefully up at me.

"I think I'd better go up and start my own homework," I said. "And Bear's ready for bed."

Will looked up from his book. "Good night, Heather," he said quietly.

Mom smiled and set up another solitaire game. "Good night."

Oh, if I could only tell! I thought. But I will tomorrow.

If Thad's right.

Chapter 14

Thought for the day: You should stand up for other people. Of course, then you may be the only one on his feet, watching the train coming down the tracks at you.

Harold Z. Zoppler, Principal
Fox Crossing High School

I could hardly wait to get to school the next morning. I rushed Bear through her walk and breakfast, and didn't even take time to pack a lunch for myself. The sidewalks were slick with ice, but I ran recklessly.

But when I got to school, Thad wasn't there yet, so I stalked the main hall impatiently, looking in the office door every time I passed to check my watch with the office clock.

Oh, hurry, hurry, I kept thinking. This is the day!

Suddenly a small riot erupted at the end of the hall. I'd seen Paige there with a group of sophomores, gathered around the bulletin board. She'd nodded to me briefly when I passed, but I knew better than to try to initiate a conversation with her. We weren't even as close as acquaintances, and I couldn't get over being sorry about it. It didn't seem to bother her much, though. And she still wore her hair as different from mine as she could.

But I was curious about all the racket, so I started walking that way. I didn't have to get very close to see what was going on.

Every Monday the week's cafeteria menu, printed on a poster, was tacked on the bulletin board. Over the heads of the crowd, I could see that it had been torn down. In its place, someone had put up a poster with a picture of a boy lying facedown in what was clearly the front entrance of the school. In red letters over the picture were the words, "I would have lived to be older if the meat loaf had been younger."

Paige stood beside the poster, grinning. I looked back over my shoulder and saw exactly what I feared the most. Mr. Stark was trotting down the hall, red faced and panting.

"You, Paige," he shouted, pointing at me. "Stop right there until I see what's going on."

I'm guilty before he finds out what happened, I thought, annoyed. But I had to get on his good side because in a few minutes, if everything went right, I'd be showing him the evidence that my stepsister had been falsely accused of cheating.

"I'm Heather," I protested mildly.

"Stand aside," he huffed. He read the poster quickly, then turned on me. "Who did this? You? When is it going to end?"

"I didn't—" I began.

"I did it!" Paige said, pushing through the crowd.

Mr. Stark saw his mistake immediately, but he wasn't about to let me off the hook. "You, Heather, did you have a part in this?"

Before I could answer, Paige said, "I told you I did it. I took the photo and we—I mean, I—had it blown up. Isn't it great?"

Mr. Stark narrowed his eyes. "We *who?* Who helped you?"

A boy named Ken Dickerson grinned. "You can send a negative to this place in California and they make up the posters, cheap."

Mr. Stark looked at him, then back at the poster. "Is that a photo of you, lying there like an idiot? I should have known. Take it down before the cafeteria staff sees it."

Ken reached up and pulled the poster off the bulletin board. The crowd was silent except for a giggle or two in the back. I could see what was coming. If the posters were cheap, there were probably others in the school, especially in the cafeteria.

Mr. Stark sighed noisily and beckoned to Paige and Ken. "Follow me," he said. He looked at me and lowered his brows. "You're not involved with this?"

"No!" I cried. "I haven't done anything for ages!"

"You're protesting too much," he said sourly. He trotted off, with Paige and Ken giggling behind him. Ken dropped the poster, accidentally on purpose, and someone darted after him, retrieved it, and put it back on the bulletin board.

How I wished that I could have been a part of the planning! But I had more serious business that day. And Paige wasn't my friend anymore.

I found Micky and Sandy halfway down the hall, watching the uproar from a discreet distance. "I thought Paige was up to something again," Sandy said.

I wasn't let in on Paige's antics now, and that hurt. "How was the dance?" I asked, to change the subject.

"Great," Micky said. "You should have come. The food was wonderful and so was the music."

"Did you get to dance?" I asked.

"Thanks a lot, pal!" Micky said, laughing. "You poked a sore place. Actually I did, a couple of times, and Sandy danced a lot."

"By myself," Sandy said, but she was grinning. "We did have a good time. I wish you'd been there. You would have seen Kix dancing with Darren and looking like a whale in a black dress."

"She was dancing with a boy," Micky said. "Who cares what she looked like?"

"Well, she looked even worse than she did last year," Sandy argued, "and I didn't think it was possible. Her brother took her when she was a junior, and I didn't blame him for not dancing with her."

"Her brother took her last year?" I asked. "That's awful. Did their mother make him?"

"Probably," Micky said. "Or she paid him."

"No, he actually likes her," Sandy said. "Lance is just like her."

"I guess I haven't met him yet," I said. "Is he a junior?"

"No, he graduated last year," Micky said. "He goes to college here."

"Here?" I asked. "In Fox Crossing?"

"Sure," Micky said. "Why? You wouldn't like him."

I was hugging myself, I was so happy. "Kix has a brother and he goes to the college. . . ."

"And he could have taken the quarterly out of the library," Sandy said. "Why didn't we remember him?"

"He's awfully easy to forget," Micky said.

I couldn't resist. I told them I was waiting for Thad and why.

They were ecstatic. "Now all we have to do is find out who could have printed that fake article and put it in the copy of the quarterly Mr. Stark has," Sandy said.

"It had to be Kix," I said. "She's the one who gave it to him."

"Is it possible that Darren doesn't know?" Micky asked.

"No way," Sandy said quickly. "Why else would he be taking her out? No, you can be sure he knows. They did it together."

"But if they don't have computers—" I began.

"We don't know that for sure," Sandy said. "Not yet."

Thad was coming down the hall. I ran toward him, reaching for the envelope he was holding out. "I was afraid you weren't coming," I told him.

"Sorry I'm late," he said. He glanced around, then said, "Are you sure you want to look at it here, in the hall?"

The hall was crowded, but I didn't care. "I can't wait," I said, and I took the copies out of the envelope.

"That's it," I said. Thad had copied the entire quarterly and stapled it together, but he'd left a paper clip to mark the article. One look at it confirmed everything he'd said. The article was about a city buried in a jungle. I showed it to Sandy and Micky, just as the first bell rang.

"I'm going in to see Mr. Stark now," I said. "I don't care if I'm late to class."

"I'd better go with you," Thad said. "I'm the one who made the copy. He might not believe you unless he hears it from me, too."

"We'll all go," Micky said. "You'll need all the support you can get, especially since he's probably in a horrible mood."

Suddenly I was scared. What if he didn't believe us? What if he thought we were just playing some sort of joke?

The school secretary was suspicious of us when we arrived at her desk and asked to see Mr. Stark. "Why?" she asked frankly. "Shouldn't you be on your way to your classes?"

"This is really important," I said.

"He's busy right now," she said.

Right. He had Paige and the poster to deal with. "Do you think he'll be finished soon?" I asked. I could hardly stand still, I was so impatient to tell him what we knew.

By way of an answer, Paige and Ken came out of Mr. Stark's office, looking somewhat chagrined but unrepentant. Both of them stared at us curiously.

"What's up?" Ken asked.

"Get along to class now," the secretary said to Ken, and he left reluctantly, with Paige right behind him.

"Suppose you tell me what this is all about?" she asked me.

"It has something to do with Tracey," I said uneasily.

She raised her eyebrows, waiting for more.

"I have to see Mr. Stark," I said. "It's practically life or death."

I was sure she didn't believe us, but she left her desk and went in to see Mr. Stark. He came back to the door with her.

"Now what?" he said. That wasn't too encouraging.

"We want to show you something," I said. "It has to do with Tracey and the scholarship."

He narrowed his eyes. "Heather, this had better not be a joke. I don't have time for any more today, especially one involving something as serious as that scholarship situation." He stepped toward me, probably hoping that he looked menacing.

"This is not a joke," I said.

We could have spent an hour outside his office door while I defended myself against something I hadn't done, so I decided to take the initiative. I marched past him, and the kids followed me. He had no choice but to follow us.

He closed the door and sat down behind his desk.

"Well?" he asked.

I handed him the photocopies. "This is the same issue of the quarterly Kix gave you. Look at the article marked with the paper clip. It's different from the article in the quarterly you have. Someone put a substitute in yours

to make it look as if Tracey had copied her essay. Someone is trying to cheat her out of her scholarship.''

He simply stared at me.

"It's true," Thad said. "I'm the one who copied the
quarterly—I couldn't check it out. But the original is in
the Perryville library. Colin and I had to go that far to
find one, because that particular issue is missing from
the Fox Crossing library and the college library, too.''

Mr. Stark blinked. "Are you sure?''

We nodded.

"Don't you see what happened?" I asked eagerly.
"Somebody wanted to make it look like Tracey plagiarized, so all the local copies of the quarterly disappeared—except for the one you have. And that one has
the fake article in it. It's got the one that's almost exactly like the essay Tracey wrote.''

"I don't need to have it spelled out," Mr. Stark said
crossly. He tugged on his lower lip and stared at each
one of us in turn.

"Why should I believe that this isn't a joke of some
kind? A very cruel joke.''

"Because Tracey's my sister!" I shouted. "Why
would I lie about my sister?''

He rubbed the end of his nose. "Why isn't Dr. Carver
here with you?''

"Because I haven't told him yet!" I cried. "I didn't
see the copy of the quarterly until just a few minutes
ago when Thad brought it to school. I didn't want to tell
my family until I was absolutely sure I could prove it.''

"Ah," Mr. Stark said. "Ah.''

"Well?" Micky asked. "Are you going to do something?''

"Are you going to call Kix in and show her this?"
Sandy said. "And Darren, too? Are you?''

Mr. Stark stared at us for a long moment. "I'll need
to check everything myself," he said.

"But . . ."

"Go to class," he said. "All of you except Heather."

"We—" Thad began.

"Good-bye," Mr. Stark said.

As soon as the door closed behind them, he leaned forward. "Now. Begin at the beginning and don't leave anything out."

I told him everything I could remember. When I was done, he looked up a telephone number and called Will at the college, asking him to come to the school as soon as he could. All the time he spoke to my stepfather, he watched me from under his eyebrows.

When he hung up, he said, "The last bell rang a long time ago. I'll give you a late slip."

"What's going to happen?" I asked while he scribbled a few words on the slip and handed it to me.

"Interesting events," he said.

"But can't I stay until my stepfather gets here? Are you going to call Tracey in?"

"Go to class," he said, tapping his pencil impatiently on his desk.

I started for the door.

"Heather?" he said quietly.

I turned around.

"What gave you the idea to check on the quarterly?" he asked.

I took a deep breath. "Of all the people I've ever known," I said, "Tracey is the most certain of what she wants. She would never take any chances on spoiling the only thing that matters to her."

"Of course," he said sadly. I could barely hear him.

As I left, I realized what I'd said. Poor Tracey. To only want one thing—to only *dare* want one thing—was terrible. And Mr. Stark knew that, too.

Chapter 15

Thought for the day: No one ever gets everything he wants, unless he didn't want very much to begin with.

> Harold Z. Zoppler, Principal
> Fox Crossing High School

I must have had a strange look on my face when I slid into my first period seat, because the teacher stopped talking in midsentence. Everybody turned to look at me.

I wanted to shout out the news, but I couldn't, not until Mr. Stark had satisfied himself that everything I said was true. And not until Tracey knew.

"Sorry I'm late," I said.

For some reason, the whole class laughed.

"Well, I am!" I exclaimed.

They still laughed.

"Would you like to take off your cap and scarf?" the teacher asked. "And maybe your jacket, too?"

Suddenly I realized that I hadn't gone to my locker that morning. I yanked off my knit cap and bundled that, my scarf, and my jacket under my seat.

"I'm ready," I said. I was past any hope of using common sense.

"Thank you very much," the teacher said wryly.

When the class was over, I found myself behind Paige as we filed out the door. I was still in such an ecstatic mood that I didn't mind taking a risk.

"That was a great poster," I said. "I hope there are

more around the school that haven't been taken down yet."

Her gaze flickered past me uncertainly. "Thanks, Heather." She hesitated for a moment. "There's another in the cafeteria on the wall that the staff can't see from the kitchen."

I grinned. "I forgot my lunch this morning, but I'll be sure to stop by the cafeteria and have a look."

She nodded and slipped into the crowd in the hall. Once we would have walked to our next class together.

Well, I thought, you can't have everything. Considering how well the day had gone so far, I couldn't complain.

Shortly before noon, I thought I saw Will going into the office, but I was at the other end of the hall and couldn't be certain. Colin and Sandy were walking with me, and Colin said that he thought he'd seen him, too.

"Do you suppose it's all over now and Tracey's got her scholarship back?" Sandy asked.

I shook my head. "It can't be that simple. Mr. Stark will have to call the people that awarded the scholarship to her in the first place."

"And have it taken away from Darren!" Sandy snickered.

"Here he comes," Sandy whispered.

I looked up and saw Darren coming toward us. I could tell from his expression that he didn't know yet that he'd been caught.

I couldn't resist. I jumped out in front of him and stopped him. "I'm taking a survey about computers," I said. "Do you use Kix's computer or does she use yours?"

"What?" He only looked annoyed, not panicked the way I wanted him to be.

"I need the information for my survey," I said. "Do

you let anyone use your computer? Or if you don't have one, do you use someone else's?''

He put out his arm to shove me aside but I dodged it.

"You didn't answer my questions," I complained.

"All right," he said. "No, I don't have a computer yet. I'm getting one for Christmas.''

"Then you use Kix's for your big projects now," I said. "Or maybe her brother helps you out. With all sorts of things.''

Now I had his attention, all of it. "What are you talking about?'' he said. His face was so white that his freckles showed worse than ever.

Gotcha, I thought. Maybe I can't prove that Kix's brother was involved, but I can sure raise the issue.

"I'll put you down on my list as an industrial-strength borrower,'' I told Darren quickly. "You know, a crook—a guy who can't get what he wants the right way so he takes it away from someone else." I started down the hall before he had a chance to respond.

Sandy and Colin ran to keep up with me. "He looks like he's having some sort of attack,'' Sandy said, laughing.

"I certainly hope it's nothing trivial," I said.

"He didn't admit anything,'' Colin complained.

"He didn't need to,'' I said. "I'd like to see him punished for what he did, but it's more important that Tracey get the scholarship back and everybody knows she didn't do anything wrong.''

"Nobody believed it anyway,'' Sandy said. "At least, nobody who knows her.''

"That's probably true," I said, "but now we've proved it.''

The cafeteria was crowded by the time we got there, and everyone was talking about Paige's poster, but it had been taken down. I was disappointed, but Thad found me and gave me some good news.

135

"Ken's taking orders for copies of the poster," he said. He draped one arm over my shoulder, dazzling me practically into a coma. "I knew you'd want one, so I ordered it for you."

"Thanks," I croaked. I was sure I wouldn't be able to talk unless he took his arm away, but if he took it away, I'd probably die.

"How did things go in Stark's office?"

"Great," I squeaked.

"I've been trying to catch up with you all morning."

"Here I am," I chirped.

He squeezed my shoulders. "I know," he whispered in my ear.

After lunch I cranked up enough courage to go to the office and find out what had been happening. Mr. Stark's secretary wasn't very cooperative at first.

"Was my stepfather here a while ago?" I asked.

She examined the point on her pencil. "I believe so."

"What happened?" I asked.

She examined the eraser on her pencil.

"I think I'm going to fall over dead if you don't tell me," I warned her.

She grinned suddenly. "Heather, aren't you going to be late for class? You wouldn't want to be the only girl in the family to be in trouble today."

"Yay!" I yelled as I ran for the door.

The rest of the day was a blur to me. All I wanted was to get home and find out every detail of what had gone on after I talked with Mr. Stark. Tracey was nowhere around after my last class, so I started off toward home alone, half running.

Thad caught up with me. "What's your hurry?"

"I've got to find out what happened today," I said.

"Slow down. Five minutes won't change anything."

I slowed to a walk. "You're right. How come you're going in this direction?"

He looked down at me and smiled. "I thought I might check on Bear."

A chill spread over me. "She's fine," I said. I'd thought he wanted to check on me!

"I confess," he said. "That was only an excuse. You're such a tough fighter that I know you wouldn't let anything happen to her. I wanted to spend some time with you. I can never find you by yourself at school."

For once I was speechless.

"Do you think Tracey knows what you did yet?" he asked.

"I suppose she knows that she's got the scholarship back," I said.

"She owes everything to you."

I shook my head. "No. You and Colin found the quarterly. Everybody helped."

"But you were the one who got us going."

"Maybe," I said. "I'm Tracey's sister so I did what sisters do."

"So you'll probably have a big celebration."

I stared at him and laughed. "Are you kidding? The Carvers never celebrate anything." I realized how bitter I sounded, and I added, "They're not very emotional people."

"She'll be grateful," Thad predicted.

"Sure," I said, and suddenly the whole thing struck me as being awfully funny. "She'll send me a small and tasteful bouquet of flowers and a polite thank you note."

Thad caught my mood instantly and grinned. "What would you rather have happen?"

I thought for a moment. "I'd rather she yelled hooray at the top of her voice and hugged me until my ribs crack. At least then I'd know that we're both really alive."

"Maybe to her, notes and flowers are just as good as yelling and hugging," Thad said, watching me out of the corner of his eye.

"Maybe I'd like to have both!" I declared.

Thad slipped his arm around my shoulders. "Here's a hug, then, in case you don't get one from Tracey, and I'll try to work in some yelling later."

Don't get me wrong—I enjoyed the hug. But I knew that it was the only one I'd get that afternoon.

Thad left me at my front door, even though I invited him in. "I have a hunch I'd be in the way," he said. "But I'll call you tonight. Okay?"

"Okay!" I said.

When I first opened the door, I thought no one was home. That was a disappointment. But I found a letter from Amelia on the hall table, so I took it upstairs with me.

Bear leaped at me the moment I opened my bedroom door, and I had to play with her for a few minutes before I could get to the letter.

Amelia begged for the latest news about Tracey, assured me that everybody had missed me on Thanksgiving, and then told me that she was getting involved in something strange and didn't know what to do about it.

I sat up straight and studied the letter carefully.

"A boy named Warren started school here in September. I don't know why I didn't write about him before. I guess it's because I'm not sure how I feel about him. He's awfully good-looking, and he's been making a big play for me for weeks. But—this sounds stupid—I'm halfway afraid of him. Do you know what I mean? There's nothing wrong wtih him—he doesn't hang around with creeps or anything like that. Honestly, Heather, I don't know how to explain this. So far he's asked me out a couple of times but I always had other plans I couldn't change. I want to go out with him—but I don't. Tell me what you think."

I folded the letter carefully and put it back in its envelope. What I *know*, Amelia, is that you should stay away from him, I thought. Just reading about this Warren made me shiver, and I couldn't have explained that to anybody but Amelia. We'd always been so close that we could practically read each other's minds.

The way Paige and I might have been if we hadn't lost the beginnings of our great friendship.

I changed clothes and got out Bear's leash. The moment she saw it, she squealed and leaped around clumsily. It was nice to have one other living creature in the house besides myself that got excited about things.

The house was still quiet when I started downstairs. I wondered when Mom and Will would come home—and where Tracey was. I didn't care where Mrs. Brier was.

But when I reached the bottom step, I heard voices, soft ones, from the kitchen. And I heard my own name.

"Heather was responsible for saving my scholarship," Tracey was saying. "If it hadn't been for her—"

"She shouldn't have meddled in what was none of her business," Mrs. Brier said.

"If I didn't know better, I'd think that you'd had something to do with my almost losing that scholarship," Tracey said coldly. "You might not have done that, but you were glad about what happened."

"I only wanted you to be here, where you'd always be safe."

"Safe from what?"

"From everything. I wanted what's right."

"But right for whom? You? It certainly wasn't going to be right for me." Tracey's voice crackled like ice. I was glad she wasn't talking to me.

Mrs. Brier was silent for a moment. "I won't have a place here when you're gone. But you'll find out that you need me and you'll be sorry when you're alone in that college clear across the country.''

''I've never needed anybody,'' Tracey said. ''I wouldn't let myself need anybody. Is that why you've been so mean to Marsha and Heather? Because you thought they'd take your place with me? Didn't you ever notice that I've never let you or anybody else matter to me after my mother left me behind? School is the only thing I care about. You hurt Marsha and Heather for nothing.''

I was sorry I'd stopped to listen, because that was a conversation that turned my blood cold. I slipped out the door, tugging Bear behind me. If I hadn't hated Mrs. Brier I might have felt sorry for her, because Tracey had just hurt her so much that I couldn't see how she could ever recover.

My mind was fixed on the picture I had of Tracey as a little girl, sitting in the park all alone and crying. And running away when someone tried to help her.

I didn't know where her mother was or what she was doing, but I hoped with all my heart that she was miserable and lonely and a total failure at everything she tried to do. For the first time I understood Tracey and why she was the way she was.

I dug a handkerchief out of my pocket and wiped my eyes, but I couldn't stop crying. It was all so terribly sad, and there was nothing I could do to help Tracey with it. Getting back her scholarship was hard enough. Getting back her awful mother was impossible.

Bear and I walked around the park twice. Most of the snow had melted, and a light rain was falling. But there'd be more snow before Christmas—everyone said that.

Christmas in the Carver house. How did they celebrate? Or did they even bother?

They'd have to bother because I was there now, and I liked Christmas trees and lights and carols. Maybe I could warm them up, Will and Tracey. Maybe I could love them until they learned that it didn't always hurt.

Well, Will loved Mom. I could tell that, and it was a start. Now if he could learn to trust me, too, and if Tracey would only notice, then maybe, just maybe, things might change.

But what if they didn't?

I sighed. Maybe families came in all types. Maybe what Amelia had—and what Paige had—was special.

But maybe other people would think that what the Carvers had was special.

All I knew was that it sure was different.

When I got home, I found Mom and Will there—and a box of flowers with a note for me from Tracey.

I buried my nose in the pink roses and did my best to hide my grin. "Thank you, sis," I said. "I love roses, but you didn't need to do this."

"I'm very grateful for what you did," Tracey said calmly. She smiled a very little smile. "You went to a lot of trouble for me."

"Heather's a true champion," Will said. He reached out as if he were going to touch my arm, but he let his hand drop to his side. I suppose that was the best he could do.

I could tell Mom was proud of me. "I always knew that the racket you can raise would come to something," she said. "Mr. Stark was impressed with you. He even said you can buy lunch in the cafeteria again."

She and I burst out laughing. Will and Tracey smiled obligingly, but I doubt if they understood what was funny.

I took Bear upstairs then, and when I came down later, I found Mom setting the table in the kitchen. A cardboard tub of take-out chicken sat on the counter.

"Where's Mrs. Brier?" I asked, astonished. I didn't know the Carvers had ever even heard of take-out food.

"Mrs. Brier is retiring," Mom said. She set another place with silverware, then suddenly looked up at me and grinned.

"I don't believe it," I said. "What happened?"

Mom bit her lip, then said, "I fired her."

"You?" I asked. "You fired her? What did Will say?"

"He said, 'Thank god.' "

I stared at her. "If he felt that way, why didn't he do it a long time ago?"

"He doesn't like to hurt people's feelings," Mom said. She wouldn't look at me.

"That's nice, but sometimes . . ."

"I know," Mom said.

"Families," I said, using my most significant tone.

"Yes," Mom said.

"They take a lot of getting used to."

"We'll manage," Mom said, and we smiled at each other.

Thad called that evening while we were having dessert in the den. We talked for a while, and then I went back to finish my cookies.

I'd had a hectic day and I really appreciated the quiet.

Chapter 16

Thought for the day: Be kind to the adults you know. They've been where you are and they didn't like it any better than you do.

> Harold Z. Zoppler, Principal
> Fox Crossing High School

Bear woke me early the next morning, eager for her walk. The sun was coming up from behind the Cascades, turning the sky pink and gold, and Fox Crossing had never looked more beautiful to me. When we got home, we found Mom and Will in the kitchen, making pancakes and giggling like teenagers over something they'd read in the morning paper. This wasn't high comedy, like breakfast at Amelia's, but it was good enough for Bear and me.

Tracey came down yawning, squinting without her glasses, and every bit as calm as if nothing had happened the day before. But I understood her—well, a little, anyway.

I was halfway through my second helping of pancakes when the phone rang. Mom answered and handed it to me.

"It's Paige," she said. "Goodness, it's been ages since she called so early."

It's been ages since she called at all, I thought as I reached for the phone.

"Good morning," I said, hoping that I didn't sound astonished.

"Can you talk?" she asked.

I looked around at my family. "Sort of," I said.

"Micky called me late last night and told me about Tracey. What you did for her, I mean."

She's angry because we didn't include her, I thought, cringing inwardly against what I was afraid was coming. "It turned out okay," I said.

"I never believed that Tracey cheated," she said.

"Neither did I," I said.

I waited through a small silence. "I should have trusted you as much as I trusted Tracey," Paige blurted. "I'm sorry I've been acting like such an airhead."

"That's okay," I said. But it really wasn't. I was having a terribly hard time with this conversation.

"I mean, I knew ages ago that you don't like Colin," she went on hurriedly. "Well, you don't like him in any special way, that is. I don't know why I couldn't call you and tell you so. I guess I'm too pigheaded for my own good."

I sighed. "So am I," I said, because it was true. "How did you finally figure everything out?"

She laughed. "You know the night Thad kissed you in the Burger House parking lot? Well, Dad and my little sisters saw you. They were coming out with their orders, and there you were."

He only kissed me on the cheek! I was going to shout, but I caught myself just in time. Will and Tracey weren't paying any attention to me, even though my face had turned red, but I could never be sure whether Mom was tuned in to my frequency or not.

"It wasn't quite that interesting," I said vaguely.

Paige laughed. "How interesting was it, then?"

"Well, I had a lot of other things on my mind so I couldn't really take advantage of the opportunity," I said.

"Will you take advantage of the next one?" Paige asked.

"Look, why don't we get together before school?" I suggested nervously. I wasn't sure if she'd accept.

"Let's get there early," she said. "I've got a surprise for Mr. Stark, and I'm dying to tell you about it."

"Another surprise? He hasn't recovered from that poster yet."

"This is a poster, too. You'll like it."

"I can hardly wait," I said, and I really meant it. "And Paige, I'm wearing the same sweater and skirt I wore the first day I saw you." I added the last sentence with my fingers crossed, hoping she'd be willing to take up where we left off.

"I will, too," she said.

When I hung up, I ran to gather up my books and coat.

"Aren't you going to finish breakfast?" Mom called out.

"No time!" I shouted. But when I came back down, I stuck my head in the kitchen door and said, "I'll eat twice as much tomorrow, if you're the cook."

Mom rolled her eyes up. "Who else?"

"There's always Mrs. Brier," Will said composedly. His gaze met mine, and to my astonishment, he winked.

"I think we're fine just as we are," Tracey said. "I can help Marsha fix breakfast." There was a trace—just a trace—of irritation in her voice.

"It was a joke, Tracey," Will said.

Tracey stared at him. "A joke? Nothing about Mrs. Brier was ever funny."

Mom and I exchanged a grin, and I hurried away. Hopeless. Well, practically.

Paige was waiting for me when I reached school. She wore the outfit like mine, but her hair was brushed the way she'd been wearing it for the last weeks. That was

145

all right. We'd find our way back to the place where we'd been before she thought that she couldn't trust me.

We had so much to tell each other that we talked right over the top of each other, but there was plenty of time to straighten everything out. I couldn't keep my eyes away from the long roll of paper she held in one hand.

"I can't stand it anymore," I said. "Let me see the poster."

She looked around. The hall was nearly empty. "Okay. But let's go over to the bulletin board because I want to put this up before the kids start coming in."

No one was near the bulletin board. I held my breath as she unwrapped the poster and held it up so I could see the photo.

I recognized Paige, wearing a shabby, ragged, witch costume, with her front teeth blacked out. She was smiling at the person who'd taken the photo, while she stirred something in a barrel, using a long stick for a spoon.

I shouted with laughter, but Paige was scowling. "Oh, darn," she said, "Dad forgot to do the lettering."

"Your dad helped you with this?" I asked.

"Sure," she said. "He went to school here. He says they're probably still serving the same rice pudding that he refused to eat ninety-nine years ago."

"What was he going to put on the poster?" I asked.

"Soup of the day."

"I'll do it," I said. "Quick, I've got marking pens in my locker."

We ran toward my locker. More kids were arriving every minute, and if we didn't hurry, there would be too many witnesses to the crime. I lettered the poster, and before the ink was dry, Paige and I were rushing it back to the bulletin board.

Thad sauntered up, grinning. "What are the Terrible Two doing this time?"

146

"Don't get involved," Paige said. "You know how hysterical Mr. Stark can be."

Thad slid his arm around my shoulders. "Oh, I'm already involved," he said.

I tried to pretend I was taking all this for granted, but I couldn't keep the absolutely huge smile off my face.

Paige and I put up the poster, then stood back to study the effect. "Perfect," I said.

"With your help," she said.

We walked off to a safe distance to watch what happened. Colin joined us, saw Thad's arm draped over my shoulder again, and shrugged. If it bothered him, he was nice enough not to show it. A few students gathered at the bulletin board. More joined them. The football coach stopped to read the poster and turned away, grinning.

Darren skulked by, without Kix. He glanced at me from under his eyebrows, snarled something I couldn't hear, and hurried on.

The first bell rang. The crowd at the bulletin board now blocked the hall. Mr. Stark emerged from the office door, redfaced and puffing. Everybody disappeared except Paige, Colin, Thad, and me. Colin took Paige's hand.

"We're not going to have this!" Mr. Stark cried. "You, Paige-Heather, take that down."

He had found a solution to the problem of telling us apart. After that he always called either one or both of us Paige-Heather.

Before we had a chance to obey him, however, someone else came out of the office, a tall, terribly thin, gray-haired man wearing a tweed suit and red socks.

"It's Mr. Zoppler," Paige whispered.

Mr. Zoppler tottered over, smiling absentmindedly at us. "Having fun, are you?" he asked in the same high, strained voice we heard each morning on the taped thought for the day.

"See what they've done!" Mr. Stark cried vexedly, and he pointed to the poster.

Mr. Zoppler moved close to the poster and studied it for a long time. Finally he said, "I know her. That's Emmaline Braithwaite. Yes sir, that's Emmaline, all right, all done up in one of her funny costumes. She married one of the Worth boys, you know." He smiled at Paige kindly. "No, you wouldn't remember that, would you? That was before you were born."

He smiled at Mr. Stark then. "Very nice poster," he said, and he tottered back to the office.

Paige grinned. "He thinks that's a picture of my mom. Wait until I tell her."

I could actually hear Mr. Stark's teeth grinding together, so I pulled down the poster and rolled it up quickly.

"Time for class," I babbled. "Come on, Paige."

We ran off before Mr. Stark got over the shock of seeing Mr. Zoppler in the hall.

At lunch, Paige shared her lunch with me. Now that we had more time, I told her about the flowers and note I got from Tracey.

"That's sweet," Paige said. "Sort of old-fashioned." She nodded for emphasis. "I like it, though."

"It's not that I didn't like it," I said. "But I could predict what she'd do. Something formal and, well, distant. Do you see what I mean?"

"Sure. And you'd hoped that she'd get all excited and shout down the house, right? I think you'll have to give up on that idea. She won't change. In some ways, I envy her. Sometimes I wish I didn't react as strongly as I do over everything."

We were both silent for a moment, remembering how she'd reacted when she thought I liked Colin too much.

"I've wished that," I admitted. "But not for long. I

don't think anybody ends up as unemotional as Tracey without suffering a lot first.''

"Like losing her mother?" Paige said. "But you lost your real dad, and you're not like that."

"I was only a baby," I said. "I don't remember my father. And even if I did, well, he died, he didn't deliberately run away and never come back. That would really hurt."

"Is this a private party?" Micky said, standing by the table with a tray. "Or can anybody sit down and complain about life?"

"Sit down and complain," Paige said. She examined Micky's tray suspiciously. "You went ahead and got the soup anyway."

"Oh, I felt a lot better about it when I saw that you were the one who made it," Micky said without cracking a smile. She tasted her soup, made a face, and said, "This reminds me—Sandy told me that there's a new horror movie in town. Do you guys want to go Friday night?"

"Count me in," Paige said.

I hesitated, thinking that there might be a remote chance that Thad might ask me to go somewhere with him. Maybe. I hardly dared hope, but I didn't want to make promises to anyone else. Then I realized that Paige and Micky were staring at me.

"Are you going?" Micky asked.

"Ah, well . . ." I began.

"You've got something else to do?" Paige asked. "What?"

"Well . . ."

Paige and Micky looked at each other. "She's got a date," Micky said.

"A real one," Paige responded.

"No, not really," I babbled.

"But you're hoping," Paige accused.

"You think you might," Micky declared.

I groaned. "I'm only daydreaming," I said. "He probably won't ask me. I'll bet it never even crossed his mind."

"We'll make our plans around you," Paige said. "Then, if it doesn't turn out right, you can go with us."

"Thanks," I breathed.

"Maybe someday you can return the favor," Micky said.

Paige looked suddenly enlightened. "Do you suppose that the guys are going to start really dating pretty soon? You know, actually asking us out instead of just assuming that we'll go along with them like good old pals?"

Micky considered this while she buttered her roll, then shook her head. "Nope," she said. "Heather will be with us on Friday."

"Pessimist," I hissed.

She blinked innocently at me. "Just playing it safe," she said firmly.

She was probably right, I thought. I'd had too many good things happen all at once and shouldn't expect anything else.

But I did, anyway.

When I got home from school that day, Bear was sitting in the front hall waiting for me. Since Mrs. Brier was gone, the pup didn't have to be shut up in my bedroom, and she was suspiciously wide-awake.

"Have you been doing something you shouldn't?" I asked her.

Not me, she seemed to say as she thundered toward the back door to be let out.

I let her out into the fenced yard, then walked around on damage patrol. Bear still liked chewing on things.

In the den, I found that she'd tipped over the waste basket. The only thing that had been in it was the copy of the article that Tracey was supposed to have copied.

I didn't know who'd put it there, but Bear had chewed it to bits. She got extra dog treats that afternoon for being so smart.

Thad came by that evening and took me out for a milk shake. We sat in a back booth so that we could talk. I wanted his ideas about getting Paige and Colin together.

"Why don't we just let them work it out for themselves?" he said. "They've been friends all their lives. If something's going to happen, it will happen."

"I'm in favor of giving it a little push."

"He liked you," Thad said. "I knew that even before he told me."

I grinned at him. "Were you jealous?"

He shook his head slowly. "No. Well, maybe a little. But we're friends. And you were the one who would end up making the decision between us. There was always the chance that you wouldn't have wanted to go out with either one of us, ever."

"Did you talk about it?" I asked, surprised.

"No. But I was sure that he felt that way, too. Like I said, we're friends."

"I thought you didn't like me because of what happened to Bear."

"I was worried about her," he said soberly. "But after a while I saw how stubborn you can be. I figured you'd be a match for Mrs. Brier."

I shuddered, remembering the awful woman.

"But everything's okay now, right?" Thad asked.

Almost, I thought. "Are you going to ask me out?" I asked, scared to death.

"I just did!" he exclaimed. "I asked you to come here."

Oh, no. It was going to turn out just like Micky and Paige thought. This was only another old-pal date. I didn't know what to say, so I finished my milk shake.

"Of course," Thad said, as if he'd been talking the

whole time and was now going to sum up his remarks,
"I'm going to ask you to go out on Friday with me,
too."

"Really?" I asked.

"There's a new movie in town. Would you like to go
with me?"

"Some of my friends are going," I said.

"I suppose we could sit with them," he said awkwardly. "If you wanted to, that is."

I shook my head firmly. "I don't want to."

"Then you'll go?" he asked.

"Of course," I said. We were getting close to the
real thing.

He slid down a little in his seat. "Boy, I was afraid
you wouldn't go."

"Haven't you ever taken a girl to a movie before?"
I demanded.

He shook his head. "No. But I suppose you got asked
out a lot in Seattle."

Should I tell the truth? I wondered. Probably it would
be a good idea. "I went out on a date once," I said. "I
spilled root beer in my lap, and he stumbled over a chair
and fell flat. And then, when he took me home, he was
going to kiss me good night but the man who lived in
the apartment across the hall came out and told him to
go home."

I could see that Thad was trying not to laugh.

"Go ahead and laugh," I said. "It cracks me up every
time I remember it."

Grinning, he reached across the table and took my
hand. "Then not everything that happens in Seattle is
perfect," he said.

"Certainly not," I told him. "For instance, I got a
letter from Amelia telling me that she might go out with
this guy named Warren who sounds like he isn't right

for her. I'd feel awful if she ended up hurt, so I'm going to write her and tell her not to do it."

"You care about everybody, don't you?"

"All my family, of course. Even my cousin Erin—and she never answers my letters or cards. I care about all special people."

"Am I one of them?"

"Looks that way," I whispered. The conversation embarrassed me a little because I was afraid people were watching us. Or listening. I pulled my hand loose from his.

He looked straight into my eyes. "Are you finally going to let yourself be happy here?"

"Sure," I said. "After all, you're here, and you're at least twice as much fun as falling down stairs. Paige isn't mad at me anymore, and before I left this evening, Will and Tracey actually suggested that you come by on Sunday for dinner. We're going to play word games afterward."

"Word games," Thad said softly, laughing.

"Be glad," I said. "Sometimes they read plays aloud. Or poetry."

I expected him to laugh again, but instead, he said, "I've got a poem for you. Roses are red, violets are blue, I'd like to go out New Year's Eve with you."

"That's an awful poem," I said. "But I think it's the best one I ever heard. I wondered how long it would take you to ask me out on a real date."

"So did I," he said, and he laughed. "Heather, when I take you home, I hope you remember that you don't live in an apartment house now. There's nobody across the hall to tell me to leave."

"I know," I said. "I can see lots of great reasons to stay in Fox Crossing."

"Are you ready to go home, then?" he asked.

"Ready to go," I said.

JEAN THESMAN was born in Seattle and still lives there with her husband and their dogs. She is the author of several novels for young readers, among them *Couldn't I Start Over?* and *The Last April Dancers*, both available in Avon Flare editions.

Avon Flare Presents
THE WHITNEY COUSINS
by Award-Winning Author
JEAN THESMAN

*Three teenage girls dealing with
the complexity of growing up—*

HEATHER   **75869-5/$2.95 US/$3.50 Can**

For Heather, adjusting to a new stepfamily and new town is tough, especially at fifteen. But when her new stepsister's honesty is questioned, threatening her chances for a scholarship, Heather pulls for her, learning what it means to be a family.

AMELIA   **75874-1/$2.95 US/$3.50 Can**

When Warren, a handsome senior, takes Amelia out and tries to force her to go too far, Amelia is afraid to tell anyone because they might think she was "asking for it." But when Warren starts bad-mouthing her at school, Amelia is shocked to find that some of her friends believe the popular senior's story and that's when she learns the true meaning of friendship.

ERIN   **75875-X/$2.95 US/$3.50 Can**

Erin Whitney's parents were killed by a drunk driver when she was ten, and she's been shuffled from relative to relative ever since. Now at her cousin Amelia's house, Erin goes out of her way to alienate her new family. But the Whitneys are a tough bunch and can see through to Erin's pain—making her feel, at last, that she has a real home.